ALEATHA ROMIG

NEW YORK TIMES BESTSELLING AUTHOR

Sinclair Duet: Book Two

A workplace, billionaire, grumpy/sunshine, second-chance contemporary romantic suspense

ALEATHA ROMIG

New York Times, Wall Street Journal, and USA Today bestselling author

2023 Edition License

Sinclair Duet, book two

In the blink of an eye, the tables turned.

I'm Damien Sinclair, a man always in control.

I thrive on the knowledge that my word is the final one—gospel.

In the millisecond I hesitated... Gabriella Crystal stepped in. I'm damn glad she did, but I will forever be in her debt.

Ella holds in her hands not only my heart, but also my future, my company, and everything I hold dear. The love we once shared is palpable, a glowing ember in the dying ash. To save my world, that ember must grow, must ignite and burst into the flames of desire.

She can never know the power she holds.

It's the only way to save all I live for.

Have you been Aleatha'd?

The Sinclair Duet is a scorching hot, second-chance romance filled with the suspense and intrigue you've come to expect from New York Times bestselling author Aleatha Romig.

*REKINDLING DESIRE is book two, the conclusion of the Sinclair Duet.

Prologue

The end of REMEMBERING PASSION

Gabriella

As Michael drove us down the winding driveway, Damien called Allen. Thankfully, he and Angie had stayed in Ashland. The pilot said he could have the plane ready in under an hour. Our first stop was our hotel.

"Don't take time to change," Damien said. "We can change on the plane."

I heard more than his words. It was as if my hearing was in tune with his soul. From what he'd shared in the past, Damien and his father had a strained history. Despite that fact, each phrase he uttered was laced with worry. Outside my room, I reached for his hand. "I'll hurry."

He looked at where we were touching and back to

my face, his expression solemn. "I don't anticipate being great company. You might reconsider the stop in Indy."

My lips curled into a smile as I leaned into his chest. "You can't scare me away after spending the last week trying to get me back."

His Adam's apple bobbed. "Thank you."

Once the plane was in the air, we both changed from our formal wear into more casual clothes. This time we were both wearing blue jeans. Damien spent most of the flight between calls with his sister and calls with Stephen Elliott, an attorney I recalled from Sinclair.

With my legs curled beneath me in the seat, I sat watching the man I'd tried to forget, seeing him in a way that contrasted the reasons I'd left him. While I'd worked for him, I'd witnessed his anger. It wasn't directed at me, but that didn't mean I hadn't heard his curses or seen the way his face could redden.

During the duration of the flight, there were bursts of cursing, yet his deep baritone voice stayed resolved, as if he was preparing himself for the worst.

I thought about Damien's offer or his proposal. It wasn't exactly the way a girl dreamed it would be. We weren't under the canopy of stars or in still water. He didn't offer me a diamond ring. Although, according to him, that had been the plan.

"We're about to land," Angie said. "There's a car waiting to take you to the hospital."

"I'm going to get my purse," I said, standing and walking to the bedroom in the aft of the plane. When I turned, Angie was behind me. "I'll hurry."

"I wanted to thank you, Ms. Crystal. I don't try to eavesdrop, but I know Mr. Sinclair is worried about his father and about the company. I'm so glad you're with him."

I swallowed. "Me too, Angie."

The memory of Damien saying the flight crew had witnessed more verbal disagreements came back. "Did you meet Amber?"

"Ms. Wilmott," she said with a serious expression. "Yes."

"I know you can't tell me anything..."

Her smile returned. "I can say we're very happy to have you back. Take care of him."

Take care of Damien Sinclair.

"I will."

Damien was still on the phone as we exited the aircraft and entered the back seat of the waiting car. The cold breezes from up north were replaced with Florida's humid air. The spring flowers were swapped with palm trees.

"He finally showed up," Damien said into the phone. He looked at me and mouthed 'Darius.'

I inhaled, wondering what the confrontation would be. It was hard to tell with Darius.

When Damien finally tucked the phone into the pocket of his jeans, he reached for my hand and gave it a squeeze. "Dad's still in surgery."

I nodded.

"I could do this alone."

"You could. You don't have to."

Palm trees lined the streets and tall lamps illuminated the way. My skin grew tight as the car came to a stop in front of the hospital. Once out of the car, Damien placed his hand in the small of my back and led me through the large glass doors. Without a word, he guided me through the hallways, up an elevator, and through more corridors.

Dani, Damien's sister, was the first person I recognized as we approached a private small surgical waiting room. She rushed from her chair and wrapped Damien in a hug.

"No word," she said, her words muffled against his shirt.

With his lips pressed into a straight line, Damien embraced his sister. The muscles in his jaw tightened as he nodded.

When Dani backed away, she turned to me. "I can't tell you how glad I am to see you."

The two of us embraced. Truth be told, she and I

had always gotten along. We'd even met a few times for lunch over the last two years. It was nice to see her out in the open.

I retook Damien's hand. "I'm glad I'm able to be."

Next stop was Marsha Sinclair, Damien's mother. When her bloodshot eyes focused on Damien, she too stood and wrapped him in a hug. "Thank God you're here." She turned to me. "Gabriella."

"Marsha, I'm so sorry about Derek."

"Are you two...?"

Before we could respond, the sound of voices caused us to turn.

"Damien," Darius said, calling from the doorway. A tall woman with blond hair was at his side. "We need to talk."

Damien's hand stiffened in my grasp. "I'm glad you're here for Dad. Nothing else matters right now." He stood taller and addressed the woman, "Amber."

Amber.

I tried not to react.

Darius was a little taller than Damien. While they were similar in appearance, Darius's hair was peppered with gray. He held tight to Amber's hand. "I have news to ease Dad's stress."

Damien inhaled.

Amber stared at Damien's hand holding mine and

then shifted her focus up to our eyes. "You two are back together?"

She obviously had greater knowledge of me than I had of her.

Before either of us could answer, Amber lifted her left hand. A diamond-encrusted band glistened under the lights. "Congratulate us. Darius and I are married."

Damien and I turned toward Marsha who nodded.

"Do you know what that means, brother?" Darius asked.

"It means you took the blackmail," Damien replied. "I'm still CEO. That's not changing. Dad will be okay."

"The addendum," Amber said.

I took a step forward and offered Amber my hand. "We haven't formally met. I'm Gabriella, Damien's fiancée."

Chapter 01

Gabriella

The halls of the hospital were quiet in the middle of the night—more accurately, in the early morning hours of Sunday. Within the small chapel, that eerie silence was but another element increasing my apprehension.

I'd made a proclamation upon our arrival to the hospital. The circumstances hadn't changed. Derek Sinclair was still in surgery. What was changing felt like an out-of-control locomotive.

Within my ears, I heard the buzzing of the warning signal.

Caution.

Caution.

It rang out, warning that we were moving too quickly.

I peered around, curious if others heard the alarm.

My mental fog lessened as I concentrated on the words of the woman before us. She held no special place in our lives, and yet she was the clergy on call—the official who would change our lives.

"...being as today is Sunday, we will have the license issued first thing Monday morning," Pastor Becky Abrams said. "In many cases, the clerk's office will postdate the license to correspond to your ceremony. Hospital weddings are a special entity—a class by themselves. Assuming the clerk's office will accommodate your wishes, your marriage will be legal as of today."

Our marriage.

"Today?" My once-strong voice was barely a whisper.

My attention went to Damien's stare, assessing the churning waters of his blue orbs. There were too many emotions swirling within the murky sea to pin down one or even two. While he had the greater burden of concern regarding his father, I wasn't a stranger to the sense of uncertainty. Within me, a conflict raged, prickling my skin and speeding my circulation with each passing minute. Contrasting emotions and feelings made my flesh taut, the tiny hairs along my skin stand on end, when all the while my insides boiled, and my skin chilled.

Damien reached for my trembling hands, holding them to his wide chest. "Ella, look at me."

My gaze moved from where he held my hands, up to his tightly clenched jaw, prominent cheekbones, protruding veins throbbing near his temples, and finally to his navy-blue stare.

"I promise a better wedding—one you deserve." His tone was deep, his promise reverberating through me as he squeezed my hands. "This one—tonight—it's just for legal purposes."

I looked around the small chapel where the three of us stood. There were no more than five rows of pews on each side. The altar was basic. A wooden cross hung from the wall, highlighted by indirect lighting. Along the side of the room was a table with candles, some lit and others not.

Biting my lip, thoughts of those I cared for flooded my mind. There was my mother, father, sister, brother-in-law, and niece. Friends also came to mind: Niles and Jeremy, Rosemary, and so many others who knew both Damien and me. I'd never dreamed of a grand wedding, yet I had imagined more than a hospital chapel in the middle of the night.

"Miss Crystal," Pastor Abrams said, her soft brown eyes taking in more than my exterior, as if she could see through to my confused soul. "If you have any reservations about going through with this ceremony..."

"It's just a ceremony? Right?"

She nodded. "The ceremony is symbolic. Once the county clerk's office opens, I'll file for the license. Signing the paper is what will make the two of you married."

My mouth and throat dried as I tried to swallow. Again, I looked up at Damien, sensing the stress that hung around him like a cloud. It was visible in the small lines around his eyes, the way his chiseled jaw tightened, and the taut muscles showed beneath his skin.

"Your dad?" I asked.

He shook his head. "We don't know. He's still in surgery."

"Sinclair Pharmaceuticals."

His nostrils flared. "The wedding could be moot."

"Or it could secure your position," I said as a new thought occurred to me. I longed to call Niles to ask him if he could hear me, if I was still present.

This marriage had been my idea.

I'd been the one to announce our engagement.

"Aruba?" I asked, recalling what he'd recently confessed.

"I still have the ring, in Indianapolis."

Sucking in a breath, I spun toward the sound of the opening door at the far end of the small aisle. Dani came rushing toward us, still wearing the clothes from hours before. She handed me a red rose tied with a ribbon and gave something to Damien.

"Surely the gift shop is closed," I said, taking the rose.

"I pulled some strings. It seems hospital security isn't unaccustomed to wedding emergencies."

Damien looked down into the palm of his hand, closed his fingers around an object, and shook his head. "No."

Dani laid her fingers over his balled fist. "Mom said she wants you to use it—to have it."

My eyes widened. "What?"

Damien forced his closed hand toward his sister. "We don't need a ring to make this legal."

"Wait," I interrupted. "Your mom can't offer her wedding ring."

Dani forced a smile. "She didn't. It isn't. The band was our grandmother's. Since Nana passed, Mom has always worn her ring on her right hand. She wants you to have it, Ella. She wants to be here, but she can't make herself leave the waiting room.

"We know this wedding is rushed, but you can't erase the years you were part of our lives. My brother is the one who needs to make this right." She feigned a smile. "Like they say, you don't only marry the person, you marry the family. Our family loves you."

I would guess Dani's new sister-in-law wasn't a fan, but maybe she wasn't including Amber in the overall family umbrella.

Sniffing, I worked to keep my emotions at bay as I looked up to Damien. "If you don't want to use it, we don't need a ring."

"I want you to have the best. A seventy-year-old band isn't the best."

"May I see it?" I asked.

Slowly, Damien opened his fingers. The ring lying upon his palm looked too small. Yet as I reached for it, I realized that it was the size of his hand that dwarfed the band. In my fingers, the band looked as if it would fit. I twisted the golden circle, rolling it between the tips of my finger and thumb. I squinted my eyes. "There's an inscription."

"Really?" Dani questioned, reaching for the band. "I never knew that." She took the ring toward a light and turned it until she began to read, "It says: Don't let the flame extinguish. Always rekindle."

For a moment, the words of the inscription hung heavily in the air.

Finally, I admitted, "I never knew your grandparents. Rekindle." The word settled into my psyche.

To relight.

To revive—something that has been lost.

"Rekindle," I repeated the word and looked at Dani. "Does Marsha really want me to have it?"

Dani nodded. "She does. Who knew Nana and Papa were romantics?"

"They sound practical," I replied. "As if they knew what it took to keep a relationship working."

"If you ask me," the pastor said, "I think they are giving timely advice from Heaven. Flames aren't difficult to ignite, whether of love, desire, or lust. A spark can turn an entire forest to ash. However, that flash is incapable of igniting the forest fire alone. The striking of metal and flint creates a flicker, yet without fuel, the spark dies. To truly ignite the blaze requires other elements. I think your grandparents' inscription means they understood that to keep the flames burning, it takes work." Her smile broadened. "All relationships ebb and flow. That is life. Taking the time and making the effort to rekindle the fire—that is what is required for a successful relationship."

The buzzing in my ears stilled as I held the wedding band. When I looked up at Damien, there were tears in my eyes.

His palm gently came to my cheek. "Ella."

On the plane to LA, he'd asked me what I would have said if he'd proposed in Aruba. My honest answer was I didn't know. That didn't mean I would have said no or yes. I truly didn't know. There was a time I imagined my forever with the man before me.

My leaving him was because I felt as if when with him, I disappeared. Maybe if he had proposed, I would have known that I wasn't invisible—that he saw me.

"Five months," Damien whispered. "If what we shared isn't rekindled, we'll agree to amicably part ways."

Part ways.

Is that possible now that we've both remembered the passion?

The clergy spoke. "I don't encourage contingency plans at a wedding."

I scoffed. Of course, she didn't. Then again, she didn't know our history. I feigned a smile. "Maybe you should. It sets a goal."

Damien nodded, the storm inside his orbs settling. "Are you ready?"

The tips of my lips curled upward as I leaned into his touch. "No, I'm not." I inhaled. "Let's do this."

Releasing my cheek, Damien's strong arms surrounded me as with a sigh, he dropped a kiss to the top of my head. Reaching for my hand, we turned to the clergy.

"Shall we begin?" the pastor asked.

Damien and I nodded. At the same time, the doors at the back of the chapel opened. We both turned. Damien's grip of my hands intensified as his spine straightened. There was no attempt at masking his displeasure. His once-supportive voice boomed, echoing through the chapel. "You're not invited."

Amber and Darius came to a stop.

"You need a best man," Darius said, "if you want to make this legit."

I turned to the minister. "Are witnesses required?"

"Not by Florida law. However, it is recommended to have two besides the notary."

"You and Dani."

Dani moved to my side. "I can be both best man and maid of honor. Just remember this, Damien, when you're sending out thank-you gifts."

While I'd hoped that Darius and Amber would leave, they took a seat in the second row. Damien, Dani, and I faced the clergy.

Pastor Abrams's voice was steadfast, a calming melody to the storms brewing in our periphery. "It brings me great joy to exercise my ability to bring two people together in matrimony. The timing isn't as important as what is in your hearts. One last time," she said, nodding toward me, "Gabriella Crystal, are you present of your own free will?"

"I am."

She nodded and turned to Damien. "Damien Sinclair, are you present of your own free will?"

"I am."

The rest of the ceremony faded into the buzzing of my insecurities and doubts. What held me tight, anchoring my feet and giving me hope, was the pastor's discussion of the inscription in the ring. It was as if Damien's nana and papa had anticipated and planned for the multifaceted being of their grandson.

Damien wasn't a man who fit into one box.

At one time, I'd feared I wasn't strong enough to be his other half.

Looking at my hands in his, I realized I was.

I was strong because I'd survived loving this man, endured remembering him, and was determined to do my part to not only rekindle our earlier love, but also our desire for one another. I wasn't going into this marriage blindly.

Damien was a man I knew well.

The usual words were spoken.

Love.

Devotion.

Desire.

There was no mention of submission, but I knew it would come—but not only from me.

Damien promised me five months.

As he slipped his nana's wedding band on my fourth finger of my left hand, I knew in my heart of hearts, I wanted forever.

Chapter 02

Damien

"**Y**ou may kiss your bride."

Bride.

The last few hours came back to me in a whirlwind of pictures and snippets of time. The memories faded as I looked into Ella's blue eyes. "My bride," I whispered.

She nodded. "That makes you my groom."

Her eyes closed as our lips touched.

My sister's applause reminded me that we weren't alone.

I squeezed Ella's hands. "You amaze me."

Possessively placing my hand in the small of Ella's back, we thanked Pastor Abrams for her time and services as she again promised to come through with the license. Turning, I met the stare of my brother.

He and Amber stood and made their way to the front of the chapel.

Darius offered his hand. "Congratulations on your marriage. Sunday wedding and all. Hope you can make it legal."

Refusing his handshake, I pulled Ella to my side. "Dad is going to recover."

He turned to Ella. "If that's the case, you chained yourself to this guy for no good reason."

"I have a good reason," she replied with her chin high. "It's called love."

Amber huffed.

That's right, bitch. The rebuttal was on the tip of my tongue. Instead, I spoke to both of them. "And I hope you're both very happy with one another. Your marriage won't secure Sinclair for either of you." I turned my stare to Amber. "And I hope you're happy with a downgrade."

Amber lunged forward, her palm striking my cheek.

Ella's body stiffened beneath my touch as Darius pulled his wife a step back, keeping his arms around her.

Without a flinch, I added, "Discussions of Sinclair Pharmaceuticals as well as the addendum are officially tabled."

Struggling against Darius's hold, Amber pressed

forward. "My mother is calling the members of the board for an emergency meeting. It's going to happen."

Taking a step closer, I stood tall. My words came staccato, seeping from between my clenched teeth. "*All*. Business. Will. Wait. Until. We. Have. More. News. About. Dad." My nostrils flared. "This discussion is over."

Darius attempted to return civility to the conversation. "As a family, we need to show unity and make a public move before consumer confidence—"

My volume rose, reverberating throughout the small chapel. "I am CEO. Dad's condition—" My hands balled to fists at my side. "This conversation is over."

There were too many things happening out of my control.

My skin felt taut as my inability to fix everything or anything ate at my insides.

I reached for Ella's hand. "Come with me."

Ella nodded as I led her out of the chapel and down the empty hallways.

I'd been in this damn hospital for more than a few days before, yet I wasn't sure where I was leading Ella until I saw the sign.

"Damien?" she questioned as I led her toward a single bathroom.

"Privacy."

Ella seemed to accept my answer.

As I pulled open the door, the rush of emotions from moments ago raced through my circulation. There was the elation that Ella was now mine in every way. That said, I couldn't ignore the nagging sadness and worry about my father. Those emotions were far from the only ones coursing through me. There was the continued shock at Darius and Amber's announcement. Rage that Amber and her mother planned to take advantage of Sinclair during this vulnerable time.

However, as Ella stepped inside the ten-by-six-foot room and I turned and bolted the door, one sensation overtook the others. Control. I needed it. I thrived on it. I'd let it slip away, and I wanted it back. Before Ella could say a word, her chin was in my grasp, my hand lifting her mouth to mine.

Wife.

Husband.

We'd both promised our 'I dos.'

Fuck yes.

She was mine.

With my world crumbling beyond the bolted door, Ella was the sun, the giver of light and life. More than that, Ella filled me with warmth. No, stronger than that. Extreme heat.

Embers that were nearly extinct since the news about my father were now a raging inferno.

My tongue sought entrance between her lips as our kiss deepened. In a matter of seconds, my hunger for this woman intensified. I was ravished, famished beyond reason. Snaking my arm around her waist, I pressed against her, flattening her breasts and grinding my growing erection against her. Small mews and moans echoed within the tiled room as our breathing hastened. Her fingers wove through my hair.

Our surroundings no longer registered.

Ella was my bride. She'd sacrificed her independence for me, for my position at Sinclair.

My future had been slipping through my fingers, and now I had a tight grip.

Tugging her top from her jeans, my hands roamed over her velvet flesh. Without thinking, I pulled the shirt over her head and dropped it to the floor. Pushing the cups of her bra down, I tweaked one nipple and then the next. Each ministration earned me a whimper.

"Wife," I growled, allowing the word to sink in.

"Damien."

With my fingers on the button of her blue jeans, I paused, lifting my gaze to meet hers. "Are you sorry?"

Ella was a vision, her blue eyes wide, her cheeks

flushed, and her lips pink and swollen. Her answer began as a shake of her head until finally her verbal reply filtered through the air. "No."

"You're fucking mine, Ella. I need to be inside you." Before she could protest, I laid my finger over her perfect lips. "In some cultures, consummating the marriage is required." I bent down, sucked a pert nipple, pulling it between my lips.

Goose bumps swept over her exposed flesh.

"I'm going to show you what you do to me."

"Your family..."

I turned us toward the mirror, the one over the sink. Within the reflection, I was far removed from the man on top of a wedding cake. Hell no. I appeared crazed. Derangement gleamed in my eyes and adrenaline coursed through my circulation. By contrast, Ella was a vision, her dark hair loose around her shoulders and her breasts on full display. "Look at us. We are the only family that matters." Reaching around her, I unclasped the button of her blue jeans and lowered the zipper. "Hands on the sink."

For a split second, Ella hesitated. My lips went to her sensitive skin behind her ear. Each word blowing a puff of warm breath onto her neck, I lowered the tenor of my voice. "Don't disobey me, Ella."

I needed this.

It wasn't an admission I could make aloud; none-theless, my silence didn't lessen that need.

Control.

Dominance.

I craved them.

Watching Ella's reaction in the mirror, I witnessed her submission. A nod. A visible shiver coating her skin in more goose bumps. Her nipples tightened, and her areolas grew a deeper red. The golden band on her left hand glistened in the artificial illumination.

"Hold on tight. Don't move your hands."

Her knuckles blanched as her grip of the porce-lain tightened.

Crouching down, I removed her shoes, one at a time. Tugging the jeans to her ankles, I pulled one leg from the pants. It was as I lowered her panties that I knew she was as willing to give me control as I was to take it.

Her essence shimmered in the bright illumina-tion, and her sweet aroma filled my senses. I pushed a finger between her folds. As the room echoed with her gasp, a smile curled my lips. "I love how wet you are."

Positioning her feet farther apart, I tugged her hips toward me, my tongue delving where my finger had just been.

"Oooh," she shrieked.

As I stood, I peppered her ass, back, and neck with kisses. Meeting her gaze in the reflection, I said, "I remember the way you liked this—stealing away for a quick fuck."

Her neck straightened as she inhaled, and yet there wasn't a syllable of protest.

Unbuttoning my jeans and lowering the zipper, I scanned from Ella's sock-covered feet to her mussed hair. Her body was perfection like no other. Kicking her feet even farther apart, I pressed her spine, lowering her torso to the sink and lined up the head of my cock with her pussy.

Yes, I wanted this, the complete control, yet I wasn't a monster. Ella would enjoy this as much as I did. One raw, animalistic thrust buried me deep inside her warm, wet cunt.

"Fuck," I growled as she called out my name.

Her pussy clamped down like a vise around me.

The last few hours disappeared as I thrust in and out.

This ritual was more than sex. It was an exorcism of the last two years. Each prod was an eraser, expunging our time apart. The fastness and fury of my fucking was Ella's punishment for leaving me. My cock glistened with her juices as I watched each time

I pulled out to the tip and pushed back in, her pussy swallowing me whole.

Our bodies covered with perspiration and audibly slapped together as I pounded, her hips banging against the sink's edge. As I reached around and rolled her clit, her body shuddered, signaling the end to the punishment.

We both reaped the reward of our reunion.

In the reflection I beheld the beauty of her bliss. The way Ella's orgasm drew her lips to a bow while her core continued convulsing and her body trembling. A few more thrusts as my fingers blanched with the pressure I was applying to her hips and the world around us exploded.

No longer in a hospital bathroom, we were floating in the bliss of the tropical Florida sky. The star-covered darkness filled with fireworks. Detonation after detonation flashed behind my eyelids as my balls tightened and my cock throbbed.

With my heart beating in double time, I leaned over Ella and peppered her shoulder and neck with more kisses. "I've missed this."

Her blue gaze met mine in the mirror. "You forgot a condom again."

Disconnecting our union, I pushed my erection back into my jeans, and reaching for her shoulders, I stood her up and spun her toward me. My cheeks rose in a lopsided grin. "Don't clean yourself. While I'm dealing with life out there, I want to think of my come on your thighs."

Ella shook her head. "I've married a monster."

Her quick response made my grin grow. "A monster wouldn't have let you come."

She lifted her fingers to my cheek. "Then what are you, Damien Sinclair?"

"Your husband. You agreed to obey me."

"I don't recall that line from the ceremony."

"Oh, it was there." I crouched down and lifted her lace panties from the floor.

Ella sighed. "I'm glad I'm wearing jeans."

Something akin to a savage possessiveness came over me as I scanned Ella's nearly naked form from her hair to her toes. "No jeans currently, and you're fucking gorgeous. Do you know what else you are?" Before she could respond, I said, "Mine." Lifting the crotch of her panties to my nose, I inhaled her sweet scent. "They're already wet. Now they'll have the combination of the two of us." I handed her the panties.

"You're a lot to handle, Damien."

Securing her chin between my thumb and forefinger, I focused on her satiated blue orbs. "You are the only one who can handle me. Physically, we fit together perfectly. Emotionally, you're my soulmate. You are now Mrs. Sinclair. There's no turning back."

"I think I meant it," she said as she situated her pert breasts into her bra, pulled her panties into place, and then eased her blue jeans up her legs. After pulling her shirt over her head and tucking it into the waist of her jeans, Ella looked at me. "Five months, Mr. Sinclair. That's how long you have to remind me why I want to stay with you. Rekindle."

I thought about the inscription. "Sweetheart, if what we just did was rekindling, in five months, we'll burn this place to the ground."

Chapter 03

Gabriella

A laugh bubbled from my throat as I looked around the small bathroom, my body still quaking from my orgasm. "This isn't exactly how I imagined my wedding day or its consummation."

"I meant what I said. In five months, I'll give you the wedding you deserve."

A million thoughts cascaded through my mind, settling on the most important. I'd married Damien. Two weeks ago, I would have called him the devil. Now, we share a last name.

Swallowing, I felt the return of the heaviness in my chest. "I feel bad about the people who didn't share our day. Your dad..." I shook my head. "My parents, Charlotte, Hunter, and Kensie." My sister Charlotte. Her husband, Hunter, and their daughter,

Kensie. "Niles and Jeremy." More names came to mind.

Damien reached for my cheek. "In December, we will invite everyone you want."

A legal ceremony.

That's what we'd done.

A real ceremony in the future.

My mom would be upset, but then again, she always liked Damien.

Inclining my cheek toward his touch, I sighed, looking into the calming waters of his eyes. "I want Derek in attendance."

Damien's Adam's apple bobbed. "Me too."

"Maybe we could keep our marriage to ourselves."

"The board will need to know, to see proof."

"We can swear them to secrecy—have them sign an NDA. That could give us five months." I sighed. "If this doesn't work, I don't want the world to know I'm divorced."

"You won't be," he said with steely determination.

"We could give my mom the illusion of planning my wedding."

"To a man she probably hates."

I shook my head. "I told my family the truth. I left you." That made me think of Damien's parents. "Oh God. Do Marsha and Derek hate me?"

"No. Like I said before, they always liked you, and

fuck, you heard Dani. I think they'd take you over me."

"What about Amber?" The question left a sour taste in my mouth.

His countenance immediately turned. "Amber is a conniving bitch. My parents know that...if you didn't catch Mom's venomous stares out there."

"I was preoccupied with the absurdity that she and Darius married."

"So are we." Damien said.

"Can we keep it quiet?"

Damien nodded. "We can try."

Lifting myself to my tiptoes, I kissed his cheek. "I'm not sorry." I scanned Damien from his hair to his loafers. Despite his messy dark-golden mane, he looked as handsome and put-together as always. Me on the other hand...

Turning on the water, I covered my palms with soap and washed my hands. The bathroom didn't appear dirty, but it was a hospital. As I dried them, I looked into the mirror, ran my fingers through my hair, and scanned over my clothes. "Do I look freshly fucked?"

Behind me, Damien grinned.

"Do I?" I asked again.

"You look radiant." Damien leaned back, his gaze going over my butt. "Nice ass. No wet spot."

I shook my head. "There is. I feel it."

I felt more than the moisture. My core was reeling from the ferocity of Damien's thrusts, and I was pretty sure my hips would be black-and-blue from the pounding against the sink. That didn't mean I wasn't also satisfied. I was—thoroughly. The anxiousness I felt as we arrived, the shock at Darius and Amber's announcement, and my qualms about our ceremony were literally fucked out of me.

He smiled. "Good."

Spinning toward him, I bathed in the glow of his smile. It was much better than the vibes he radiated on the plane and during our arrival. Lifting my hand to his cheek, I said, "You're obnoxiously confident."

Taking a few steps, Damien backed me up until my shoulders collided with the tile wall. "I'm confident that knowing my come is inside you makes me hard." His menacing smile grew. "I like the idea of it there—on you, your thighs...and the other night, all over your stomach and tits."

After the orgasm I'd just had, it seemed impossible for Damien to take me from satiated to horny in a matter of seconds, but if I was honest with myself, his cocky response was turning the dial, twisting my insides, and reminding me how great it felt to be at his side. Swallowing, I feigned being unaffected. "If you're trying to get me pregnant, it won't work." I ran my hand over my left shoulder. "I still have the implant."

"When is it due to be replaced?"

Squinting my eyes, I tried to remember. "End of this year."

The blue of his eyes twinkled. "Coincidental timing."

"One step at a time."

Taking a step back, Damien removed his phone from his jean pocket and typed out a text. His navy stare met mine. "I'm texting Dani. If nothing has happened with Dad, I say we go to the cafeteria and by the time we return, the hickey I left on your neck won't be as red."

"What?" I said loudly, spinning toward the mirror and lifting my hair. My eyes searched my reflection.

"I'm kidding."

His phone buzzed.

He shook his head. "Nothing new. Let's go get a cup of coffee."

As I turned to unlock the door, a rush of heat washed through me. "What if someone sees us coming from this bathroom together?"

"They'll obviously know we fucked."

"Wait. What? There could be other reasons that the two of us..." No, he was right. They would know. "Okay, stay in here. I'm going out first."

Damien reached for my hand. "We're walking out of here together with our heads held high. You, my dear, have the unique ability to calm me. You did that because before we came in here, I was ready to punch my brother. Your method of calming me is no one else's business." He left a kiss on the top of my head.

My chest warmed with his assessment.

I'd calmed him.

A romp in a public bathroom was a small price, especially with the orgasm I had, when it came to seeing his sexy smirk.

"Here goes," I said, turning the bolt and opening the door.

After I peered out right and then left, the empty hallways filled me with a sigh of relief.

Damien led me toward the elevators. With his hand in the small of my back, we waited for an elevator.

"There you are. You both disappeared."

The two of us turned to Damien's sister.

"I just texted you. Has anything changed?" Damien asked.

"Nothing about Dad. I checked on Mom. She's obviously stressed. Could I talk to you two?" She looked around. "Privately?"

Damien took a step back and nodded. "We were going to the cafeteria. Join us."

As Dani nodded, the happiness she'd displayed in the chapel was replaced by the stress and worry of the last week. Her hair was piled on her head in a haphazard bun. She wasn't wearing makeup, and her clothes were soft and comfortable. It was the dark circles beneath her bloodshot eyes that were the most telling.

None of us said a word as we descended to the ground floor. As we walked toward the cafeteria—both Damien and Dani seemed to know the way—we made small talk.

The Florida humidity.

Our dislike of hospital coffee.

A distrust of Darius and Amber.

Entering the cafeteria, Dani looked around at the tables. Given the late—or early—hour, most of the tables were empty. "Good," she said. "I was afraid Darius and his new bride would be here."

"They're not with Mom?" Damien asked.

"No, I haven't seen them since your ceremony."

"I'd say that it's shitty to get married while this is going on," Damien said with a glance to me.

I shrugged before reaching for Dani's hand. "That makes us shitty too."

"No," Dani said definitively.

Damien stuffed his hands into the front pockets of his blue jeans. Uncertainty showed in his expression as he changed the subject. "My mind is a mess. Days are blending together. How long has Dad been in surgery?"

"Going on six hours." She looked from me to Damien and back to me. "Thank you for keeping him sane."

"Wait a minute," I replied. "I didn't sign up for safeguarding his sanity. That would definitely require a renegotiation of terms and compensation."

Dani smiled. "You two work out the details. I'm just saying you obviously have a positive effect."

We stepped into the food area. The grill station was dark and empty. Only prepackaged food in an open refrigerator was available. Scanning the choices, I remembered the delicious meal at the Shermans' home.

It seemed as if it had occurred weeks ago, not hours.

Forgoing food, we made our way to a row of coffee pots, each of us filling a cup. I added cream to mine. Dani skipped the cream and added sweetener. Damien drank his black.

"You might add sweetener," Dani recommended. "It's really bad."

"I remember from last week," Damien replied.

After Damien paid the cashier, the three of us found a table near large windows. The scene beyond the panes and palm fronds was a parking lot filled with cars. Tall light posts cast circles of illumination through the darkness and down to the pavement below.

Dani's eyes narrowed and she straightened her neck. Looking at her brother, she insisted, "I support you, but if you don't tell Ella about the addendum, I will."

"Fuck," Damien growled.

Demanding was definitely a Sinclair family trait.

I lifted my hand. "I know."

Dani turned her tired eyes to me. "You know?"

"I do. It's why I said we were engaged." I shrugged. "Damien had asked earlier today. I hadn't answered him until then."

"You know and you went through with the wedding?" Dani asked.

Laying my hand on Damien's knee below the table, he covered mine with his. "The addendum isn't the only reason I went through with it," I admitted.

After a smile, Dani rolled her eyes. "You know that's why Amber married Darius."

"We assumed," Damien answered.

Dani let out a long breath and leaned back. "Apologies, brother. I didn't trust you to be honest and forthcoming."

Damien scoffed. "As long as Ella does."

"I do." *I think*. I didn't say the last part.

Dani lifted her paper cup to her lips. Before taking a drink, she murmured, "Amber is a bitch."

At least there were a few things these two siblings could agree upon.

"Do you think they're really married?" Damien asked.

"I haven't seen a marriage license, but that ring on her finger says they are."

"Fuck," Damien cursed under his breath. "I need to speak to Stephen. Amber said Gloria is calling a board meeting." He stood, scooching his chair over the tile. "Dad doesn't need to know any of this. I'm still CEO." He pulled the phone from his jeans pocket. "I'm putting an end to this farce."

Before Damien walked away, I noticed the return of his stress showing in the way his temples throbbed, his jaw turned rigid, and the tendons in his neck tightened.

"I'll be back."

We watched Damien walk toward an empty section of the cafeteria.

Once he turned away, Dani reached for my arm. "I'm sorry I didn't speak up earlier about the addendum. This night has been a series of clusterfucks. Are you sure you're okay with marrying him? I don't want you hurt—again. Explain what's changed between the two of you?"

Meeting her stare, I sighed. "I'm not sure I would classify my wedding as a clusterfuck, but in hindsight it was the cherry on the top." I lifted my coffee to my lips. "As far as what's changed, honestly, I'm not sure."

She tilted her head.

Inhaling, I stared for a moment into my cup, watching the caramel-colored liquid. By the time I again met Dani's stare, she was still patiently waiting for my answer. I lowered my voice. "You know I didn't leave him because I didn't love him."

She nodded.

For a moment, I chewed my lower lip. "I wanted to forget him. Forget how much love we shared...and the passion."

Dani smirked, the gleam in her eye reminding me of her brother's. "Are you saying my brother is hard to forget?"

"Impossible." I exhaled, relaxing my shoulders. "I care about him, Dani. I promise." I lifted my gaze to where he was standing, still talking on his phone. "Right now, he's about as vulnerable as I've ever known him to be. Is it wrong I want to help him?"

She shook her head. "Help him, Ella. Don't change your expectations, and don't expect to change him."

"Maybe I've changed," I surmised, thinking aloud. "Not my expectations, but who I am. I think I have." I wasn't the woman he dated years ago. I wasn't his employee. The parameters had changed. "I know how hard he works. Darius doesn't deserve to be put in charge of Sinclair Pharmaceuticals. If I can help Damien, I want to."

"What does that mean?"

"I guess it means we will work to rekindle what we had."

Dani nodded.

"Everyone's focus should be Derek," I said, repeating what Damien had said earlier.

"I support you both," Dani said. Looking down at her phone, her eyes widened. "Mom said she wants us all upstairs right now."

Right now.

There was no stopping the onslaught of dread in Marsha's summons.

Chapter 04

Gabriella

The coffee in my paper cup quivered in my grasp as Damien, Dani, and I stepped from the elevator. The echo of voices was our first clue that Marsha wasn't alone in the waiting room. There was a man in blue scrubs standing before her. I reached for Damien's arm.

Am I offering him my support or am I seeking his?
Both.

That was what a true partnership was about.

Dani rushed ahead, standing at Marsha's side as Damien and I grew close enough to hear the doctor.

"...the next twenty-four hours are critical. A second heart attack in such a short period of time was not something we wanted to see. The good news was that Derek was here when it occurred. He received immediate care..."

Tears slid down Marsha's cheeks as Dani reached for her mother's hand.

The doctor looked around the room and feigned a smile. "Derek has a loving support system here with all of you. We plan to keep him intubated and unconscious for the next twelve to twenty-four hours. As you can imagine, the opening of the chest once is painful. Twice is excruciating. Right now, he can't feel the pain. Once he can, that pain can cause an increase in blood pressure.

"Our goal is to ease him back to consciousness while managing the pain. It's not unusual for patients to wake frightened, irritable, or confused. As I said after his first surgery, Derek's initial response upon waking is not indicative of his permanent mental state. At this time, our focus is on regulating his medications, monitoring his vitals, and finding the combination of medications and treatments that will work best for him.

"Currently, he is on anticoagulants to thin his blood, making it easier for his heart to pump. These medications can lead to other problems." He took a deep breath. "I'm not going to sugarcoat this. Your husband" —he looked around— "and father has a long road to full recovery."

"He has a road," Damien said. "He will recover."

The doctor nodded. "Statistically, he should. I'm

not God. I can't relieve every fear you're experiencing or alleviate the worries you'll have if you research his condition online."

"How long will he be hospitalized?" Marsha asked.

"If all goes well, he should be moved to the rehab floor in a few days."

As the doctor spoke, I held tightly to Damien's arm. Beneath my touch, his muscles flexed. My thoughts went back through the years to when Damien and I were together. I recalled Derek from the office and also in more personal settings—dinners, celebrations, and visits.

Marsha nodded. "Thank you."

I must have missed the end of the conversation.

Marsha took Dani's hand in hers and reached for Damien's. "I'm glad you're both here. I know you both have work to do, and your dad knows that." She squeezed Damien's hand and stared up at her son before turning to me.

Her gaze went to the band on my left hand and up to my face. Before I could speak, a smile curled her lips and moisture came to her light-blue stare. "Congratulations. I'm sorry I missed your wedding."

Holding my ring finger on my left hand with my other hand, I nodded. "You and Derek will be present for the real ceremony."

She reached for my hand and squeezed. "I'm

having trouble thinking beyond the here and now. Ella, Damien needs you and you're here. That's what matters to me." She turned to her son. "Regarding Sinclair Pharmaceuticals, do what you need to do. I don't want your dad dealing with any more stress than necessary. Finalize the CEO status and stop Darius in his tracks. I know you can do it especially with Ella at your side."

A lump of emotion formed in my throat as I swallowed. "He won't be alone."

Damien's deep voice came strong and assuredly. "I'll take care of Sinclair, Mom. You and Dad don't need to worry."

Marsha nodded.

"And Dani," Marsha said, "I've spoken with Stephen. Tomorrow he'll have papers for me to sign, temporarily giving you your father's and my voting power. I'm not leaving his side, but I want you to go back to Indianapolis with Damien and Ella. We are a family and" —she took a ragged breath— "we will not be seen as weak or wounded. Your father would never forgive himself."

"Mom," Dani said, "if I go, you'll be alone."

Marsha shook her head. "I'll be with your father."

Dani wrapped her mother in an embrace as tears blurred my vision.

Before I knew it, I was holding Damien's torso

and his arms were around me. Beneath my ear, his heart beat a steady and strong cadence. I'd venture to guess that Marsha had heard the same thing in Derek's chest not too long ago. I peered upward and took in Damien's features—his furrowed forehead, prominent cheekbones, firm lips, and chiseled jaw.

With a sigh, I laid my head on my husband's chest.

Derek was alive.

He'd survived the second surgery.

Darius and Amber had started a full-out coup, an attempt to steal Sinclair Pharmaceuticals from Damien and ultimately from Derek's second family. The weight of all of the above washed over me as I closed my eyes. The coffee I'd drunk did very little to slow the exhaustion circulating through my veins.

Damien's words vibrated in his chest. "I want to see him before we leave."

I didn't need to open my eyes to know the conflict Marsha was enduring. Her husband was near death for the second time. The company he'd run for most of his life was being used as a pawn in a sick game of power, and she wanted her children happy.

After Marsha promised to do her best to get both Dani and Damien back to Derek's room, Damien led me to chairs where we'd been seated hours ago.

Hours.

My tired mind couldn't compute.

Days had passed or weeks.

"We'll get a hotel," Damien's voice was a rumbling whisper. "That way we can get some sleep and come back to the hospital before flying back to Indy."

"Not too far away."

"I'll text the driver."

"All our luggage is back in the plane," I said, aware that Damien's proclamation for his come on my thighs was my current situation.

He nodded as he typed into his phone. After a few minutes, his phone buzzed. Tipping his head toward mine, he said, "The driver has our suitcases and will be here in less than half an hour. Johnathon secured us a suite nearby."

"What about Dani?" I asked, seeing she was still across the room with Marsha.

"She's been here since his first surgery. She has a room."

Nodding, I whispered, "I don't recall ever being this tired."

A quick look at my watch told me that we'd awakened twenty hours ago in Ashland, Wisconsin. The reaffirmation of our long day added weight to my arms and legs as we stood.

"Mom," Damien said, garnering her attention.

"Ella and I are going to get some sleep. We're not returning to Indianapolis until after we come back, and I see Dad."

"If you see your brother, please tell him to do the same." She looked at her daughter. "I want Dani to do the same. I'm going to your dad's room once I'm given the go-ahead. There's no sense in any of you staying here."

"If you want Darius gone," Damien offered, "I'll make sure he's gone."

Marsha's lips pressed together and her nostrils flared. "There's nothing good he can do at this time. I want your dad excluded from the talk of CEO."

"I won't say a word."

"He did." She took a ragged breath. "Darius called Derek yesterday evening." Marsha had all of our attention. "Your dad was agitated, and it wasn't long after the call that the alarms began to sound."

Beneath my touch, a tenseness returned to Damien's body.

My husband's voice cooled. "I spoke to Stephen a little while ago. This farce is done. If Darius calls, intercept the call or text."

Marsha tilted her head. "Thank you."

After a quick goodbye to Dani, Damien and I walked to the elevators hand in hand. It wasn't until the doors closed that I looked up at him. "Nothing about your dad's health is your fault. If anything, it sounds like it was Darius."

Chapter 05

Damien

I'd blamed myself for Dad's first heart attack based on what Darius had said. My conscious mind knew my brother was wrong, yet I couldn't stop the nagging subconscious feeling that my decision to reappropriate funding away from quarterly dividends was part of the reason Dad was fighting for his life.

Ella's hand came to my chin, turning me toward her. "It's not your fault."

I clenched my jaw with the realization she was right. Dad's health wasn't my fault. That didn't mean I couldn't lay the blame for Dad's latest episode on my brother. As the doors of the elevator opened on the first floor, my gaze met that of the man in my thoughts.

Surprise registered in his orbs while simultaneously, mine heated with rage.

Releasing Ella's hand, I balled my fingers into a
fist and swung.

Pain radiated from my knuckles to my shoulder as
my fist collided with Darius's left cheek.

"Stop." The repeated screams of our wives echoed
through the hospital lobby yet did little to slow my
attack.

There wasn't time to think or consider who was
watching as Darius took a step back and I followed
with another punch and another. Each strike offered
a means of release. Fucking Ella in the bathroom had
settled my nerves; that was, until Mom told us about
Darius.

Down on one knee and holding his face, Darius
raised his other hand. "Stop," he mumbled.

Despite the time being in the middle of the night,
two uniformed guards rushed our way. It wasn't until
one spoke that I saw he was brandishing a sidearm.
"Take a step back, sir."

Stretching out my fingers of my right hand, I
backed away and spoke to the heavyset man with the
badge and gun. "My name is Damien Sinclair. My
father is on the sixth floor. This man is barred from
visiting. I want him barred from the hospital."

"You can't do that," Darius said between curses.

Amber reached for his elbow, helping him stand. After shifting his jaw one way and the next, he spoke again. "My name is Darius Sinclair. I have every right to see my father. He's currently in surgery."

The guard slowly placed his gun back in the holster. "You two are coming with me."

Ella reached for my arm. "Sir, we're all tired. We're sorry for the disruption."

He narrowed his eyes at her. "And you are...?"

"Gabriella" —there was a slight pause— "Sinclair. My mother-in-law has asked that Darius stay away."

"Marsha wouldn't do—"

"She did," I snapped, cutting off Darius.

"I could press charges," he said. "I should."

I took a step closer to him. "What did you say to Dad yesterday evening? His second heart attack is because of you."

"That's bullshit. I told you last week he was upset about what you were doing..."

The second hospital guard stepped between Darius and me. His movement reminded me of a short referee stepping between two much taller basketball players. The guard held up his hands. "Both of you leave." He turned to me. "I'd like to get your mother's name. We'll sort this out."

I nodded, ignoring the throbbing pain in my hand.

The same guard turned to Darius and Amber. "Visiting hours are over."

"My father is in surgery."

"He's not," Ella replied. "He's out, and the next twenty-four hours are a waiting game."

"You can't stop us—" Amber began.

"I can," the first guard said. "The lot of you. Take this outside. I don't want to see any of you back in here until cooler minds have prevailed."

"I want to press charges," Darius said. "Physical assault. A police report."

"Do it, brother." The words seeped from between my clenched teeth. "I'll see your physical assault and raise you attempted manslaughter."

"Dad's still alive."

"Attempted," I repeated.

"Come on," Amber whispered, tugging on Darius's arm.

The first guard nodded.

The second guard, turned to me with a small tablet. "If you could give me the information on your parents. I'll check with your mother."

"Check with her," I said. "As soon as I leave here, I'm hiring a security firm to keep her and Dad safe." I looked up to see Darius and Amber near the front doors. "They'll also make sure he doesn't get near either one of them."

The guard sighed as if he'd heard the same story before—as if I was some blowhard making claims I'd never be able to take to fruition. What he didn't know was that I could hire the best team. I'd have them in place before dawn.

"Your mother's name?"

"Marsha Sinclair," Ella said. "Her husband, Derek Sinclair, is only recently out of surgery."

"Sixth floor? Cardiac."

We both nodded.

He looked down at my hand. "The emergency room is that way." He cocked his head.

I shook my head. "Keep my brother away. I'll have a private security team here in a few hours."

"We'll talk to Mrs. Sinclair and follow through on her wishes." His forehead furrowed as his eyes opened wider. "May I suggest some rest? Your family is dealing with a lot at the moment, and it can be exhausting." He looked around. "There are cameras."

I didn't have time for this shit. I narrowed my gaze.

"We'll take care of the footage, Mr. Sinclair. We were informed of your father's admission. Keeping the identity of our patients safe is part of our job. We don't need this shit on social media. Nothing happened here."

Inhaling, I snaked my arm around Ella's waist, and nodded. "Thank you, Officers."

Ella and I walked in silence toward the front doors. With each step, I wondered if Darius would be outside on the sidewalk, waiting for his second hammering. Through the rotating door, we were met with a wave of humidity. Even though it was somewhere around three in the morning, my skin beneath my clothes quickly covered with a film of perspiration.

"No Darius," Ella said.

A large black Suburban pulled up to the sidewalk. After parking, the driver got out and came around. "Mr. Sinclair. Ms. Crystal."

"Mr. and Mrs. Sinclair," I replied as he opened the back door.

"My apologies."

"Not necessary." I helped Ella into the SUV. "Do you have our luggage?"

"Yes, sir."

I climbed into the seat at Ella's side. "Just get us to the hotel."

The slamming of the car door cut off the sounds of the night. Sirens in the distance disappeared. The faint sounds of birds and insects were gone.

"You're not doing a good job of keeping our marriage secret," Ella said with a tired grin.

I scoffed. "Secret-keeping gets lower on my priority list the more tired and pissed off I get."

She reached over and laid her hand on mine. "Are you suggesting I use this time to learn all your dark secrets?"

As the driver took his seat behind the steering wheel, I turned my left hand so we were palm to palm. Lowering my voice, I whispered, "Dark secrets can wait. Ask me what I want to do to you when we get to the suite."

Ella pressed her lips together and shook her head. "Some ice for your hand, a cool shower, and sleep."

My eyebrows moved up and down. "I'm liking the shower idea."

"You're incorrigible."

I lowered my voice to a deep growl. "You're mine now, Mrs. Sinclair. I don't plan on letting you forget."

Pulling my phone from my pocket, I found Johnathon's number and hit call.

"It's too early," Ella protested.

Johnathon answered before the second ring. "Mr. Sinclair." His voice was as clear as it would be in the middle of the day.

My gaze met Ella's. My next phrase was more for her than Johnathon. "Sorry about your sleep. I have a list of things I need done before sunrise."

"What do you need?"

Once I hung up the phone, I met Ella's judging stare.

"You never called me in the middle of the night like that. He needs a raise."

"I never called you because in the middle of the night you were at my side...next to me, beneath me, over me...And for the record, he's well compensated."

"I'm not even going to start on salary inequality."

"Good," I replied. "I'll text Mom and tell her about the security, and then it's the two of us in the hotel."

"I'm exhausted."

I lifted her hand and brought her knuckles to my lips. "Our wedding deserves more than a quick fuck in a public bathroom."

"It's not legal until we sign the license."

"More days to celebrate."

Chapter 06

Gabriella

*L*ooking down at my left hand, I spun the gold band beneath my knuckle as Damien unlocked the door to our suite.

Ours.

It seemed inconceivable that two weeks ago, I was living my best single life and keeping the memories of Damien at bay. My heart accelerated, beating faster as he opened the door and pushed our luggage inside.

He flashed a tired grin my direction. "I should carry you over the threshold, Mrs. Sinclair."

Before I could respond, my feet left the floor as Damien lifted me, cradling me against his hard chest. Despite my wavering thoughts, my lips curled, causing my cheeks to rise, and a giggle bubbled from my throat. Once inside the suite, Damien's lips took mine before he lowered my feet once again to the tile.

Light trickled through the unblocked windows from the central Florida city beyond. Tipping his forehead to mine, Damien secured my hands in his. "I can't believe you're here with me, that you're officially mine." He lifted my left hand and ran his finger over the ring. "It's as if this last week has been both a dream come true and a nightmare."

I pursed my lips, hearing the sadness in his tone. "Derek will be okay."

Damien nodded.

"As for this week," I began, "I'm also having difficulty comprehending it. I think I'll fall asleep and wake up in my condo, shaking my head that I could concoct such an outrageous dream."

"You didn't say nightmare."

Shaking my head, I grinned. "Whirlwind. The only nightmare part is watching your anguish over your dad and Sinclair Pharmaceuticals."

"Darius," Damien growled.

Taking a step back, I found the switch and turned on the overhead light. My focus went to Damien's right hand. His knuckles were red and swollen. I gently ran my fingertips over numerous small lacerations. "Does it hurt?"

"I'm fine," he reassured.

"I think ice is needed." Turning toward the suite, I took in the space in for the first time. The turning on of the light made the large windows appear black, reflecting what was within. The suite was larger than our respective rooms in Ashland. To the left was a small kitchen, with mini appliances and a round table. Straight ahead was a living area with multiple sofas, chairs, and tables. Centered within the windows were glass doors that led to a balcony. Off the living area were two frosted French doors. Through the open doors, I saw a large king-sized bed within the bedroom. "I could call for room service, or maybe..." I headed toward the kitchen. Opening the freezer of the slender refrigerator, I found two ice trays filled with ice. Pulling them from the shelf, I announced, "Just what the doctor ordered."

When I turned, Damien was there, mere inches away. His deep voice resonated through me. "You, Ella, are all the doctor ordered." His left hand came to my cheek as his lips met mine. He tasted of coffee and exhaustion, yet his approach was far from that of a tired man.

Up on my tiptoes, I met his kiss with equal fervor. Our kiss deepened as we leaned into one another. Were we reassuring each other that this was real? Or were we seeking the connection we'd once had? Whatever we were searching for, our exploration took us from the kitchen to the bathroom, our clothes littering the floor, leaving a trail in our wake.

The mirrors covered in steam as we stepped inside the glass shower.

Heated water rained down, washing away the extraordinarily long day. With a soapy washcloth, I left suds as my touch roamed over Damien's wide shoulders and down his torso. He forced his fingers to bend as he massaged shampoo and conditioner through my hair.

With my fingers splayed on the tile wall, I felt a sense of loss as he cleaned my core and thighs.

As if reading my mind, he lowered his lips to my ear and whispered, "I'm not done. You'll be marked again before we fall asleep."

With a grin over my shoulder, I peered up at the mountain of a man who was now my husband. My heart wanted bows, flowers, and candies. My mind knew our future wouldn't be that easy. There were mammoth obstacles in our path. However, in my state of sleep deprivation, I clung tightly to the idea that we would make it beyond the five months to a happily ever after.

True to his word, Damien filled me with his seed, once under the warm spray and again in the soft large bed. By the time my eyes finally shut, sunshine was peeking around the heavy curtains.

I woke disoriented, as if life was a film I was watching in slow motion.

My senses came to life.

Touch was the first—soft sheets against my skin. All of my skin. I was nude.

Hearing came in a close second—the rhythmic sound of measured breathing reminded me that I wasn't alone.

Smell registered—the fresh scent of bodywash and the floral aroma of hair products.

Sight caused my eyes to squint. Even with the drapes closed, the room was bright.

It was touch that had my attention.

Warmth.

Radiating from the man at my side.

My long hair was no doubt in unruly waves from falling asleep with wet hair. As I turned and lifted my head, I was mesmerized by the realization that Damien was my husband.

My pulse quickened at the memory of the pastor declaring us wed.

For longer than I would admit, I watched my husband in slumber.

A force of nature, Damien rarely appeared less than in control of any and every situation. Yet here he was, sound asleep. His full lips were parted, his dark-blond mane wavy, and his body relaxed. Seeing him this way was striking and reassuring at the same time.

I longed to snuggle close, to bring my lips to his, and to peer beneath the blankets to learn if he was sporting a morning hard-on. I'd willingly help him if needed.

Morning.

What time is it?

Searching the room around me, I found nothing. No phone. No clock. No indication of the time of day other than sunlight seeping from behind the curtains.

What if Marsha or Dani had tried to call?

Quietly and with no sudden movements, I eased myself from the bed. Our luggage sat untouched in the living room where we'd left it. Within the depths of my purse, I found my phone. The only missed calls were from Niles.

Sighing a breath of relief, I searched for Damien's phone.

Success came within the pocket of the jeans he'd worn the day before.

Nothing I tried could wake the phone from its sleeping state. I supposed it was much like Damien himself, for once taking time to rest. Being the same brand of phone as mine, I quietly found my charger in my suitcase and plugged in Damien's phone.

After a trip to the bathroom and back, I chose the warmth and security of the bed, at my husband's side.

My husband.

Curling close to him, I drifted off.

Time was irrelevant.

The next time my eyes opened, there was no disorientation. I woke to a husky voice, strong arms, and an erection probing my lower back. "Fuck, this is the best way to wake."

If given the opportunity, I would have agreed. However, my mind was too consumed by the lifting of my behind. A yelp came as I was filled in the best way possible.

There was no wondering about Damien's morning status or if he needed help. It was I who clawed at the sheets, trying to stay earthbound.

Chapter 07

Damien

Morning sex.

The best fucking way to start a day.

My thoughts were consumed by the woman in my bed, the softness of her skin beneath my fingertips and the way her pussy spasmed around me, strangling my dick while creating the best mind-blowing torture. Everything about Ella was perfection, from her soft mews to the way she screamed my name as she was falling apart. A few frantic thrusts more and my orgasm hit with the power of a barreling freight train. Stars exploded in supernovas as I let out a loud rumbling roar. With my heart beating in double time, I slowly did the one thing I didn't want to do— disconnect our union.

Ella rolled beneath me, her shining blue eyes stared up at me, and her smile grew. "I agree."

Lying to her side with my elbow on the pillow and my head held by my fist, I felt a twinge from the damage I'd done to my right hand. Stifling a grimace, I asked, "Pray tell, what do you agree with?"

Ella scooted up against the headboard and took my right hand in hers. "Oh, Damien, we never put ice on this." Her nose scrunched. "It looks a little better. How does it feel?"

I stretched out my fingers a couple of times. Each assertion ached, yet everything moved, making me relieved I hadn't broken anything. That wasn't true. I would be happy to learn I broke my brother's nose. "I hope it feels better than Darius's face."

With a scoff, she shook her head before placing kisses on my bruised knuckles. "You could have it looked at today at the hospital."

Hospital.

"Fuck." I spun and flung back the blankets. "What time is it?" Standing fully nude, I turned this way and that, looking for my phone as simultaneously, the world beyond our bubble came crashing down upon my shoulders.

"Your phone is plugged in by the desk."

Plugged in.

I couldn't recall plugging it in last night, or before we fell asleep.

By the time I reached for my phone, Ella was beside me, wrapped in a sheet. In the middle of my mental chaos, she was standing before me, a Greek goddess. Laying her fingers on my arm, she explained, "I woke up earlier and checked both of our phones. I couldn't get yours to respond so I plugged it in."

I let my phone die.

That was something I'd never do, had never done.

Fuck.

"I'm supposed to be the one taking care of you."

"That's not completely true," she said with a grin. "I'm not a delicate flower in danger of wilting."

"You're not. I still like taking care of you." My smile returned. "Dressing you." I teased the sheet from her breasts. "Undressing you."

"I like that too. I also like taking care of you. I know you want the world to see you as invincible. Remember, I know you. I can love you for your obstinate alpha ways and also for a man who is better with me by his side."

Her words faded as the screen of my phone came to life. "It's after one."

Sunday afternoon.

This had to be the longest day in the history of days.

Ella's eyes opened wide. "Shit. Is there any news

from the hospital?" She turned toward our luggage. "What time is checkout?"

"We didn't indicate we were leaving today," I mumbled as I took in the number of missed calls and text messages. Instead of reading, I hit the icon next to my mother's name. As her phone rang in my ear, I met Ella's worried gaze. The room around us stilled; only the hum of the air conditioner was present. Finally, Mom answered.

"Damien, where are you?"

My free hand ran over my mussed hair. "Fuck, Mom. Asleep. I haven't slept like that in..." I looked over again at Ella. "...in a long time. How is Dad? How are you? Is the security team there?"

"Your dad is still sleeping. His blood pressure started to go up. The nurses said it was probably from pain, so they increased his pain medication." She took a ragged breath. "I'm looking at the monitors now. His numbers are better."

I let out a sigh of relief. "That's good to hear. What about the security?"

"They're here. A man named Conner introduced himself to me. He promised to keep Darius and Amber away." She sighed. "Oh, your father would be furious, but I won't put up with the tension. There's too much."

"If Dad is upset, he can be upset with me. I don't

give a shit." I scoffed. "Fuck, let him be mad. That means he's doing better."

"I love you."

My voice softened. "Love you too, Mom."

"How is Ella?"

My cheeks rose. "She's perfect." She was no longer standing in the doorway. I could hear sounds coming from the other room.

"Tell her thank you."

"Thank you?"

Mom's voice sounded lighter. "If you slept that well, I bet she had something to do with it."

"She did. We'll be to the hospital as soon as we can."

"Damien, you should go back to Indy. Your dad is as steady as he can be. Dani is waiting for your call. We met with Stephen this morning. Danielle has voting proxy for Derek and me. Gloria has called a board meeting for nine o'clock tomorrow morning."

"Fuck," I growled, my grip of the phone tightening.

"You take care of Sinclair. I know you can."

My head was buzzing as I clenched my teeth. "I will."

"Keep me informed."

"Will do. Bye."

Ella was back to the doorway to the living area,

her arms crossed over her breasts and the white sheet still her only clothing. "Your dad?"

"Same. Mom said they upped his pain meds."

"What upset you?"

"Gloria Wilmott called an executive board meeting for nine tomorrow morning."

Ella inhaled and nodded. "What do you think our chances are of pulling some strings at city hall?"

"What strings?"

"We need our marriage license, and we need it today. I don't know many court clerks who work on Sunday."

I eased a bit of the pressure on my molars.

Pulling strings.

Getting favors.

My life was spinning out of control, but I still had tricks up my sleeve—well, if I was wearing sleeves. "We're getting that license today."

"You sound confident."

"As confident as I am that tonight, you'll be screaming my name back in Carmel."

Ella snagged her lower lip with her teeth. "I'm not sure about cohabitation. I mean...five months, remember? Keeping this marriage a secret."

Stepping closer, I lifted her chin. "You're mine. Today we'll have the license to prove it. I don't give a damn if we're at my place or yours. As of sometime early this morning, they both became *ours*."

She opened her eyes wide. "Can Stephen postdate a prenup?"

I stood taller. "A prenup? Are you protecting your assets?"

"Yours."

Pressing my lips together, I shook my head. "Tell me, did you marry me for my money?"

Ella's smile turned sultry. "Yes, and for your cock. Especially for your cock."

"We'll work this out. One thing at a time."

"I didn't marry you for your money," she said, "and I'm willing to sign a prenup to prove that."

I tugged at the sheet as the rich aroma of coffee awakened my taste buds. "I'll make you a deal."

Ella gasped as the sheet fell to the floor. "Damien."

"Walk that sexy ass over to the coffee while I call Johnathon and get things moving with the marriage license."

"That's not a deal. What do I get?"

"My cock whenever and wherever you want it."

She hummed and tapped her finger on her chin, pretending to think over my offer.

"Oh, one more thing," I said as I leaned down to give her a kiss. Just as quick, I reached for her elbow and spun her away. My hand landed with a loud slap to her ass.

"Ow," she squealed as she jumped away.

"Now I get to watch that sexy ass with my handprint in bright red."

Her eyes sparkled as she backed away from me. "You used your right hand. Did it hurt?"

"Like a motherfucker."

"Good." She turned back around, swaying her behind and giving me the view I wanted.

Chapter 08

Gabriella

I wasn't sure how Damien did it, but he did. At three o'clock on a Sunday afternoon, sitting on the sofa in our hotel suite and staring into the camera atop Damien's laptop, we met with a Hillsborough county clerk. As if our middle-of-the-night ceremony wasn't obscure enough, we were meeting with the county official via Zoom.

It seemed that even the county clerk would make exceptions to rules. Our license was postdated to last Friday. I had no doubt that his wallet was a bit thicker for his flexibility.

By the clerk's image, he was seated in front of a green screen that looked like a quintessential courtroom. In reality, I would guess he was at his pool or in his lanai on a Sunday afternoon. There were probably swim trunks below the shirt and tie.

After uploading our Indiana driver's licenses, paying the nominal fee, and answering a few questions, the license was issued.

"Thank you again for your time," Damien said. His dark-blond mane was no longer messy. His toned abs and muscular shoulders, as well as his earlier erection, were now covered, hidden beneath a layer of clothing. Dark blue jeans covered his long legs and a white button-down shirt with rolled sleeves finished his attire.

We'd secured a first-aid kit from the hotel. Damien's hand was coated with antibacterial ointment and was wrapped in white bandages.

"Your license should arrive to your email in a matter of minutes. Remember to have the officiant sign. Once that signed license is returned to our office, you will receive your completed license via mail."

"We appreciate your help," I added as a knock came to our hotel door.

Damien squeezed my knee. "That should be Pastor Abrams now."

As Damien said goodbye to the clerk, I went to the door.

"Mrs. Sinclair," Pastor Abrams said with a smile.

"Getting closer to making that legal by the minute." I gestured into the suite. "Please come in."

Damien stood and greeted Pastor Abrams. "Thank you for coming on a Sunday afternoon."

"You were able to get the license...I didn't want to be the cause of a delay." She tilted her head. "How is your father?"

"He's a fighter."

The pastor looked at Damien's bandaged hand and to me. "Like father, like son."

A grin lifted my cheeks. "When a Sinclair wants something done, it most usually happens."

"If you'll excuse me," Damien said. "I need to go to the business center to have the license printed. I'll be right back."

After brushing my cheek with a kiss, Damien disappeared into the hotel hallway.

"May I get you something?" I asked. "A water bottle? I'm afraid we don't have much of a selection."

"I'm good. Thank you." She went to the sofa and took a seat. "While we have a moment, I wanted to talk to you about something, if you don't mind."

If she wanted to talk about our marriage, I was more confident in our decision than I was last night. After a good night's sleep and a few orgasms, I was ready to defend our choice.

Smoothing the skirt of the cream-colored sundress Damien had delivered while I was showering, I sat in a nearby chair. "What do you want to discuss?"

"The couple that entered the chapel at the beginning of your ceremony...?"

That wasn't what I expected.

I sat taller. "What about them?"

"I had the sense that there is animosity between that man and Mr. Sinclair."

"They are both Mr. Sinclair. Brothers."

"Oh," she said. "I see. I debated mentioning something I observed to Mr. Sinclair...yours. I was concerned about the safety of his family. However, if that gentleman is his brother, I must have misunderstood."

"What did you observe?"

She pressed her lips together. "You have to understand, it isn't my place to tell tales."

I pressed forward. "Whatever it is, it must be bothering you, or you wouldn't have mentioned it."

She took a deep breath. "I almost didn't recognize him—as the man from your ceremony. His face was swollen and bruised. I was in the emergency room early this morning after your wedding. He was waiting to be seen, and I was drawn to him. When I introduced myself, he didn't mention that we'd met earlier or even his name. We spoke about his injuries."

"Did he tell you how he was injured?"

"A mugging outside the hospital."

Interesting.

I nodded.

"You weren't surprised to hear he was injured," she said.

"Darius is a grown man. I'm sure he can take care of himself."

"That's the thing. Before the doctor arrived, a man entered Darius's...? That's his name?"

"Yes."

The pastor went on. "This man who entered, I didn't recognize from the hospital. He identified himself as security and demanded that Darius leave the hospital. I tried to intervene. He was obviously in need of care."

"What happened?"

"They exchanged words. A security guard, one I did recognize, joined the discussion and told the patient to leave. The woman...she was with him earlier."

I nodded.

"She came in during the discussion. Before they left, I heard something about getting what they deserve. I believe I heard them mention your husband's name." She inhaled. "A moment ago, I saw the bandage on your Mr. Sinclair's hand. I can't help believing the two incidents are connected and honestly, the other couple was very upset. In my line of work, it isn't always weddings. I see many revengeful and dangerous people. It was a feeling. I wanted to warn you to be careful."

"They are connected," I admitted. "From what I know, Darius is more bark than bite." However, I knew next to nothing about Amber. Could she be vengeful? I sat taller. "Thank you for telling me. I'll definitely inform Damien."

As if summoned by his name, the door from the hallway beeped and opened.

"Later," I whispered.

There were too many current concerns for me to give Damien another. I willingly took on the role of his wife. If he could juggle all that he had going on and still manage to get me a dress for my marriage license signing, I could investigate what Darius and Amber had planned.

Entering the suite, Damien held up a piece of paper. "We are a signature away."

I forced a smile, unwilling to let Darius or Amber ruin what little remained of our wedding.

Pastor Abrams took the paper and scanned the information. "It all seems to be in order. With the license dated Friday, we'll put Saturday's date for the ceremony. It will raise fewer questions."

"As long as it's legal," I said.

"It is." She pointed to the line above my name. "Sign here."

Taking the pen in hand, I scrolled Gabriella Louise. I stopped. "What last name do I sign?"

"On the license, you sign your maiden name."

I nodded and wrote *Crystal*. Meeting Damien's stare, I handed him the pen. "Your turn."

"That's the last time. From this day forward, your name is Gabriella Louise Sinclair."

"Maybe I'll choose to use my maiden name."

He smirked as he signed his own name. "We can discuss this after our guest leaves."

Recalling the sting of my behind from earlier, I said, "If you're offering me a deal, I think I need to work on my negotiation skills."

Damien handed the pen to the pastor. "You're the last signature."

She signed her name. "There. You are official. I'll take this to the clerk's office personally in the morning."

Damien pulled out his phone. "Let me take a picture of it." He snapped a photo. As we said goodbye to Pastor Abrams, Damien handed her a white envelope. "Thank you again for all you've done."

"You don't need to..."

Damien gently pushed the envelope toward her. "Our appreciation. Keep it, donate it. The choice is yours."

Pastor Abrams nodded. "Thank you both. It's been a pleasure." She looked at me. "Stay safe and well." She smiled at Damien. "Your father will be in my thoughts and prayers."

"Thank you."

After she left, I asked, "How much did you pay her?"

"Having you as my wife is priceless."

"How much?"

"Enough to guarantee she follows through on filing the license tomorrow." He looked around the suite and back to me. "You're beautiful, Ella. I wish I could take you to a tropical paradise." He teased a strap of the dress. "Where clothing is optional."

"I like the dress. Thank you again."

"I told you that I like dressing you. Your suitcase was packed for Ashland, Wisconsin, not Tampa, Florida. I didn't want you succumbing to heatstroke before you signed that paper."

"My hero."

"We both know that isn't true." He took a step closer, wrapping his arms around my waist and tugging me to him. "Ella, this wedding has been so much less than you deserve. I promise to keep my word and give you the most lavish wedding you can possibly dream of once life settles." He took a deep breath, his chest pushing against my breasts. "I don't want to keep our marriage a secret."

I stiffened in his arms. "Damien, I don't want to be divorced."

"Neither do I." He smiled a lopsided grin. "Rekindle. Pastor Abrams was right about a lot of things she said."

"What did she say?"

"Our contingency plan is in place, but we shouldn't concentrate on that. She also said to be open and honest. I'm being honest—I want the whole fucking world to know we're married."

Open.

Honest.

"So, keeping something from one another this early in our marriage isn't a good idea?"

"If it's that you're not wearing panties, I think we can fit a fast fuck into our schedule."

I playfully slapped his shoulder. "Yes, I'm wearing panties. I don't want to fly back to Indiana with your come on my thighs."

His navy orbs sparkled as his eyebrows danced.

"No," I said definitively. "Are we ready to go back?"

"The driver will first take us to the hospital. If we

can't see Dad, at least we can see Mom. Also, Dani is going to meet us there and fly back with us."

Dani.

Did she need to know what Pastor Abrams told me?

I needed to tell Damien.

"Before we go, I should tell you something the pastor told me."

Chapter 09

Damien

We were hardly in a private office. Instead, it was a small consultation room off a larger waiting room on the sixth floor of the hospital.

"We found him in the emergency room," Leo Conner said. A tall, thin man, he was the lead on the security team I'd authorized to watch over my parents. "I'd already spoken with the hospital security." He shook his head. "It wasn't difficult to get Mr. Sinclair out of the building—just noisy. He could have made it easier on himself."

Everything the man said coincided with what Ella shared earlier—the story she'd heard from Pastor Abrams. The information I didn't know was what I would ask next. "Where is he now?"

Leo slowly shook his head. "Sir, my team was

hired to keep Mr. and Mrs. Sinclair away from your parents, not to monitor their movement."

"Did you hear him or his wife say anything that could be construed as threatening?"

"They were both pissed. I didn't give their words that much consideration. People like to rant. It's not unusual in our line of work. It's mostly bluster."

That wasn't the answer I wanted.

Leo continued, "I have two other members of my team besides myself on this job. If you want more, say the word."

This wasn't the location that worried me. The pastor's story had gotten to Ella. I could hear the change in her tone. She tried to sound strong, but damn, marrying me wasn't supposed to come along with the threat of violence. The more I thought about the possibility, the more I knew that if Darius or Amber did anything to harm or frighten Ella, it would be the last damn thing they ever did.

"I want to hire more people," I said, "not for here. You have a good team. Mom said you met with her."

It wasn't a question, but Leo nodded with a 'yes, sir.'

"My wife" —damn that sounded good— "my sister, and I are flying back to Indiana, where we live."

"I read your parents were from northern Indianapolis."

A smile threatened my gruff exterior. "A man who does his homework. I like that. Now, if there is even an inkling that my brother and sister-in-law may pull something to retaliate, I want Ella and Dani to have around-the-clock bodyguards."

"Our company can provide that kind of security, but I need to warn you, it's expensive."

"Find me four of your best men or women. I want them in my office in Indianapolis tomorrow afternoon. I'll interview them and decide on the best two."

"If I may," he said. "I've worked as a personal bodyguard on multiple different assignments. I'm certain you know what you're looking for, but the assignments that work the best and have the best results are the ones where the client is involved in the hire. Your wife and sister must feel comfortable with this person, or they won't work well together. And working together is what keeps people safe. Full disclosure of location at all times. It's when someone decides they can sneak away for an hour or two that everything goes to hell."

Sneak away.

Yeah, I could see both Ella and Dani trying to pull that shit.

"I guess that means I need to tell them what's happening."

"How long do you anticipate needing these bodyguards?" Leo asked.

"Open-ended. Get me the particulars, and tomorrow we'll interview."

"Yes, sir."

I added, "If you have any further encounters with Darius or Amber Sinclair, I want to be notified immediately." The executive board was scheduled to meet tomorrow at nine. "I have every reason to believe they'll be in Indianapolis tomorrow. After that, I don't know. Unfortunately, my brother has the means to travel when and where he wants."

Spoiled fucking rich kid with hurt feelings and a wife willing to fan the flames.

"Do you still want us working the hospital?"

I nodded. "Yes. My mother deserves the peace of knowing you're here."

"Very well, sir."

Ella peered through the narrow window within the door before turning away.

Standing, I offered Leo my hand. "Thank you for taking care of my parents. I'll look forward to hearing from you about tomorrow. Send the bios on the four prospective bodyguards by tonight."

Leo nodded as we shook hands.

Opening the door, Leo stepped out as I scanned the larger waiting room. Clusters of people sat here and there. Mom wasn't here. She was in Dad's room, undoubtedly watching his monitors and learning everything she never wanted to know about cardiac recovery.

To my right, down the hallway, I turned to see Ella and Dani coming my direction.

"Any news?" I asked as they came to a stop.

"No," Dani said. "Mom promised she'd call or text."

"Let's head back to Indy."

Ella offered a slight grin as she reached for my arm. "Do you want to talk to your mom again?"

"No. She knows we'll fly back down if needed."

Dani lowered her voice. "Thanks for the security, Damien. Mom won't say it, but she feels better knowing Dad won't get upsetting visitors."

"Yeah, she said it to me. I told her if Dad gets pissed, tell him I did it."

"It's what I've always done," my sister said with a laugh.

Securing Ella's hand in mine, I asked, "I want to know what you're thinking. I can see the wheels turning."

Ella shook her head. "There are too many things to

pin down one or two. I was thinking about my new campaign. I'd jumped in with both feet, and now I haven't thought about it since we left the Shermans' house." She grinned. "I'm hoping the boss at my new office will accept my excuse. I've had a crazy weekend."

"I hear he is a real dick."

"Oh," she said, "he can be."

Dani chimed in, "He sounds like someone I know."

Getting to the plane and into the air was uneventful. I spent most of our flight going through the information Johnathon had provided. I had the numbers to back up my appeal to the executive board. Gloria may have thought blindsiding me during my father's medical crisis was to her advantage, but truth be told, I had the possibility of a coup in my head for the last five-plus years. I never imagined it would involve Amber Wilmott or marrying Ella.

Darius didn't stand a snowball's chance in hell of taking over Sinclair Pharmaceuticals. The numbers didn't lie. Since launching propanolol, our net earnings were higher than ever in our history. Under my leadership, we've put more money into research and development while still maintaining our market share of our tried-and-true formulas. Even without the addendum, Darius would be hard-pressed to make a case for his reinstatement as CEO.

As we drew nearer to Indianapolis and while Dani was on a call, I convinced Ella to accompany me to the back bedroom.

Though she came willingly, once the door shut, she placed a fist on her hip. "I'm not being fucked with your sister out there."

It wasn't what I'd planned. Nevertheless, I wasn't one to back down from a challenge. Step by step, I made my way to my wife. Still wearing the off-white sundress with her hair high on her head, she was breathtakingly stunning. Add her little declaration of limitations and I was growing harder by the second.

"Damien," she said, keeping her blue stare on me.

"I can compromise. A blow job."

"What? No."

Cupping her cheeks, I brought my lips to hers. When our kiss ended, I tipped my forehead to hers. "I'm worried about you."

"Don't be." Her hands came to my chest. "You have too many things to worry about. I'm fine."

Not exactly a glowing declaration from a recently married woman.

I took her hands in mine. "I wanted to talk to you about something first before we tell Dani."

"That sounds serious." Ella sat on the edge of the

bed. "Don't ask me to make any life-altering decisions. This weekend has turned my mind to goo. You
see, I left Friday morning to go on an unexpected
business trip, and now I'm returning a married
woman." She looked down at the gold band.

"You've seemed quieter since you told me what
Pastor Abrams said about Darius and Amber."

With her lips together, Ella nodded. "I've been
thinking about it, but Damien, don't worry. I am
fine."

I took the seat at her side and reached for her
hands, covering them with one of mine. "I love you,
Ella. I have. I never stopped. We don't know our
future, but I can promise you, they will not hurt you
or anyone I care about."

"If they were mad about being asked to leave the
hospital, imagine how they'll react tomorrow when
we prove that we're married. Their game will be over.
You won, Damien. I don't know Amber well. Hell, I
don't know Darius that well, but I can't believe that
they'll walk away and admit defeat. They married
with your dad in critical condition." She shrugged.
"We did too."

"You're probably right about them not going
quietly."

"What will that mean?" She swallowed. "I don't
want to think about what they could do."

"Nothing," I said adamantly. "There is nothing they can do. At the hospital, I spoke with Leo Conner. He's the head of the security team I hired. He works for a much larger company. Tomorrow, four prospective bodyguards are coming to my office. I want you to be there."

Her forehead furrowed. "Bodyguards? For you?"

"No, for you and for Dani."

Ella hopped from the bed and paced back and forth. "A bodyguard. No. That's crazy. I'm just me. I'm not a celebrity or someone who needs a bodyguard."

Following her to my feet, I reached for her shoulders, stopping her movement. "Who you are is Mrs. Gabriella Sinclair, only the most important person in my life. I have five months to prove to you that we belong together. Allowing my brother or his crazy wife to get near you isn't an option. Leo recommended that you and Dani be involved in the hire. He said that it's important for the bodyguard and the client to work well together."

She lowered her chin and sighed. "I don't want this."

I kissed her hair. "It won't be forever. I need your help."

Slowly she lifted her chin and met my gaze. "My help, with what?"

"How you just reacted...Dani will be ten times more against this. I need to do this. I need to know the two of you are safe. Help me convince my sister she needs a bodyguard."

"That's not fair. You're asking me to convince her of something I myself don't want."

I lifted her chin. "But you'll do it because I want it."

"Marriage is supposed to be fifty-fifty. I'm feeling a little cheated on that percentage."

"You're right. I owe you. I'm willing to pay my debt in full. To do that, you need to be safe. Say you'll help me."

"Is it too late to ask Pastor Abrams to tear up the license?"

"Way too late," I said. "You're mine. I'm not letting you go."

Chapter 10

Gabriella

Every single argument Dani had against hiring bodyguards, I agreed with. That said, I kept my word to Damien and argued his side of the debate. By the time we landed in Indianapolis, the discussion was over. After tomorrow's board meeting, Dani and I would join Damien in the afternoon to contribute our opinions toward the hiring of our bodyguards.

"Join us for dinner?" Damien said to his sister as we waited for the cabin to open on the tarmac.

She shook her head. "I want to get home. Besides, you two are newlyweds. You don't need a third wheel."

Third.

I scoffed. "After tomorrow, it seems we'll have five —wheels."

Dani reached for my arm. "Your mission is to convince this overprotective oaf that the bodyguard thing is overreach." She winked. "My money is on you, Ella."

Looking up, I met Damien's resolute stare and shook my head. "I think we should accept the inevitable and enjoy tonight as our last night of freedom."

"For fuck's sake," Damien said as there was an audible pop from the opening door, and fresh warm air drifted into the cabin. "I'm not putting the two of you in prison."

Dani smiled. "We could riot."

The creases near Damien's eyes and the tight muscles in his cheeks told me more than his words. I reached for his hand. "First, we should concentrate on tomorrow's board meeting."

He nodded. "I'd say our marriage is our ace in the hole, but it's not. Darius and Amber know about it. I'm sure Gloria does too."

We continued our conversation as we descended the steps and walked toward the two waiting cars. With the sun still high in the evening sky, the heat of the day radiated in waves over the blacktop tarmac. Yet as I lifted my chin to the summer breeze, the lack of humidity from Florida was refreshing.

"What do you think Darius and Amber have?" Dani asked. "To bring to the board."

Damien's jaw clenched. "I don't know. I've been racking my brain. If their only play is Darius and Amber's marriage, we already have them trumped. They know that. Why call an emergency meeting?"

"Because of Derek?" I offered.

"That doesn't require a meeting," Dani said. "An email of his status is sufficient."

Damien inhaled. "I think we have to be prepared for anything."

"I'm glad we have it narrowed down," Dani said. "Try to get some sleep. I'll see you both at the meeting."

"I can't attend," I said. "I'm not a member of the executive board."

"Of course you can," Damien said. "You're my wife and now a shareholder. You're also our liaison with Beta Kappa Phi. You can explain the advantages of the campaign and how we anticipate that relationship increasing our consumer revenue."

"Wait, you want me to talk and give a presentation? Tomorrow at nine in the morning?"

"I think you should be prepared."

I shook my head. "Thanks for the advance warning."

The driver opened the door to the back seat of the SUV.

"You're welcome," Damien self-contentedly replied as he helped me into the automobile.

I waited until the door was closed before turning to my husband. "Seriously, you could have said something earlier. I would have spent my time on the plane going over my notes from this past weekend."

"I didn't think of it until just now."

"You are impossible to work for. This is why I thought being the campaign manager on this project was a bad idea."

Instead of responding, Damien's smile grew.

"What are you so smug about?" I asked.

His answer didn't come in words as he reached for the back of my neck. Pulling me toward him, his lips took mine. Possessive and strong, he continued his advance. Our faces turned as we gasped for air. It was as the car began to move that I pushed against his hard chest. "That wasn't an answer," I managed to say, my lips still tingling from our encounter.

"It was."

"A kiss is inappropriate during discussions of work."

He shook his head and lowered his voice. "Nothing is inappropriate, Mrs. Sinclair. You're now officially mine. I reserve the right to kiss you anytime

I want." His hand came to my knee and slid beneath the skirt of the sundress.

Using both hands, I stopped his progress. "Damien."

His smile quirked. "What are you thinking about?"

"You," I said in exasperation. "How could I be thinking of anything else?"

"Name the companies in the coalition."

I shook my head. "What is this, a quiz?"

"Name the companies."

Fine. I rattled off the list, "Sinclair, Wade, Broche, Moon, Perry, Holston, and McCree."

"What is the goal of the campaign?"

"To increase awareness of said companies among medical facilities in exchange for the coalition's support of Beta Kappa Phi."

Damien sat back with a sigh. "Ella, you're naturally amazing. I hadn't thought about you addressing the executive board before, but even if I didn't mention it until the meeting, you could still pull a presentation out of your sexy ass."

Turning toward the windows, I reflected on what he'd just done. Admittedly, I felt better about the board meeting than I had a few minutes ago. I turned back. "Speaking of asses, you can be a real pain in it sometimes."

"Be careful, Mrs. Sinclair. I'm once again imagining my handprint on yours."

I shouldn't let his sex-laden comments get to me. I shouldn't be as easily distracted by the twinkle in his navy orbs, the possessiveness of his kiss, or the thoughts of the pleasure from the sting of his hand.

A sane woman would put a stop to his ways.

It was official: my sanity disappeared the moment I announced our engagement.

Our driver continued his silence as he navigated traffic, taking the familiar intrastate toward Carmel.

"Where are we going?" I asked, knowing I wanted to go to my house.

"First stop is our place."

I scoffed. "Not narrowing it down."

"My place. It's pretty much as you remember it. I'm going to pack a few days' worth of clothes and grab a few things from my office." He lowered his volume. "And then the next stop is our place, formerly yours, where I'll get to see my two favorite pussies."

Shaking my head, I grinned. "Duchess will be happy to see you."

"What about my other favorite pussy?"

"Oh, you know...trying to keep up with your insatiable hunger."

He lifted my hand, entwining our fingers. "It is, after all, our honeymoon."

Once we pulled up into the driveway of Damien's house, I was struck with the realization we were married. A little late, I was aware. It was seeing his massive home that made the marriage real.

Stepping out to the pavers, I stared up at the beautiful house located in a prestigious small subdivision. I remembered when he bought the house. With four bedrooms and six bathrooms, it seemed huge—too much house for one man.

The driver helped Damien with our luggage, getting it inside the three-car garage before bidding us goodbye. We'd discussed earlier how Damien would drive us to my place.

"I'm surprised you've kept this big house," I said as he opened the door leading into the massive kitchen. "I don't think of you as someone who enjoys lawn care."

"They're called gardeners, and I pay them."

"It's still a lot of house."

His gaze met mine. "Maybe I never gave up on why I bought it in the first place."

I looked around at the pristine white cabinets, quartz countertops, and custom light fixtures. "I always loved this kitchen. Cooking in here was like cooking on one of those TV shows." As I ran my fingertips over the cool countertop, I thought about his answer. "What did you never give up on?"

Damien took my hand and led me through the kitchen out into the two-story living room, complete with a stunning fireplace that went all the way up to the ceiling. Without a word, he continued up the stairs with the wrought-iron banister to the landing that looked down into the living room. It wasn't until we were in the primary bedroom suite that he finally spoke.

Lifting his hand, he said, "Stay right where you are."

I stood with my sandals on the plush carpet, swaying the skirt of my sundress as he walked to a tall chest of drawers and opened the top drawer.

It was as he removed a small box that my heart began to beat in double time.

As he turned my way, there was a turbulent new sea of emotions in his orbs with a spark of sunshine breaking through the clouds.

"Ella," he said, his deep baritone voice reverberating through the cavernous room. "Nothing regarding our wedding was right or what you deserved. I wish with everything in me I would have offered this to you that starry night in Aruba."

Tears filled my eyes.

This was silly. We were already married.

Maybe my emotions were too discombobulated to concentrate on our mixed-up timeline.

"Damien," I said, my voice cracking.

Falling to one knee, Damien opened the small box, revealing a gorgeous round diamond solitaire on a white gold or platinum band. Simple and stunning. "I never gave up on us, Ella. If you remember, I bought this house a few months before our trip to Aruba. I had it all planned out."

"You never let on."

"Maybe we needed time apart to realize that we belong together."

Swallowing my emotions, I nodded. "The ring is beautiful."

"I bought it for you. After you left, I refused to think about it. I couldn't bring myself to take it back. I also couldn't imagine it being on anyone else's finger. Ella, this ring is yours. I'm yours. You're mine. Even though we've said our vows, you deserve to be asked the question: will you marry me?"

"I already did."

Standing, Damien kissed me. A sweet and gentle sign of affection. It didn't hold the same power as the kiss earlier in the car. Then again, he wasn't trying to distract me. The kiss was a prelude to him sliding the diamond down my fourth finger, resting on top of his grandmother's band.

"They don't match," he said. "We'll get you a new band."

I shook my head, staring down at the rings. "They're beautiful together. I don't want another band. This one is special. It was your nana's, and Marsha wanted me to have it."

"It's your choice."

"They're perfect."

Damien looked around the bedroom. "I'll pack a few things to take to your condo."

"I guess the good news is that we can drive to the office together."

"Walk around and refresh your memory with the house. We can decide which place we should call home."

There wasn't really a choice. My condo was less than 2000 square feet. If I remembered correctly, this house was nearly 6000 square feet. As Damien packed his things, I made my way around the other bedrooms and all the way down to the lower level, the one below the first floor. A smile spread across my face as I recalled Damien's excitement about this large room. With a wet bar that could be advertised as a second kitchen, a large screen television, exercise equipment, and a pool table, this man cave was all he said he wanted in a home.

I glanced down at my left hand.

He wanted more than that.

He wanted me.

"Ella," Damien called from the main floor.

"I'm down here." We met on the staircase. "What is it?" I asked, seeing the concern in his expression.

"Van just called. He'd called earlier, but with Dad...I hadn't returned his call."

My mind swirled with possibilities. "Is everything all right with Julia and the kids?"

"They're fine. It's something he learned about Dwain Welsh."

"From Moon Medical?"

"I think we've discovered Darius and Amber's plan."

Chapter 11

Damien

Everyone's attention turned to Ella and me as we entered the large conference room on the second floor of Sinclair Corporate Center. The room had been set up for the emergency meeting. By the expression on Gloria Wilmott's face, she wasn't surprised to see Ella at my side. She wasn't in the minority.

"Damien," Lynwood Sharp, the board's parliamentarian and longest standing member greeted us as we entered. With a smile and a nod, he offered his hand to Ella. "Mrs. Sinclair, it's nice to see you again."

Ella didn't fumble. She was in her rare and unique form, the woman I observed at the Beta Kappa Phi gala.

"Mr. Sharp. I've missed so many familiar faces."

Lynwood slapped me on the shoulder. "Congratulations, you two. Sorry to miss the wedding."

"It was small," Ella replied.

Lyn's smile dimmed. "How is Derek?"

Following Stephen's advice, I made a point of contacting the members of the board last night, a short phone call to personally reach out about Dad and to let them know Ella and I had married. As we progressed around the room, I believed it had been the right move. We weren't surprising Darius; we shouldn't surprise anyone.

The room was beginning to fill.

Only the members of the board could vote on any proposals, yet stockholders were welcome to participate in the debates. Sinclair was a private company with less than one hundred stockholders. If everyone showed to each meeting, we'd need a bigger room.

Dani entered.

She was a stockholder.

What many didn't realize was that the paperwork she and Mom had executed gave Dani the power of both our parents. That not only meant two votes, but it meant she could legally sit in Dad's position as chairman of the board.

Yes, he was retired, but his chairmanship kept him involved.

"Damien," Gloria said with a nod.

Ella squeezed my arm. "Excuse me, I'm going to speak with Dani."

I laid my hand over hers for a moment.

Once she was gone, Gloria went on, "I'm sorry that it has come to this. With the unknown status of your father, we can't wait any longer."

"My father's status isn't unknown. He's stable and under the care of competent medical personnel. Tell me what couldn't wait."

"Some alarming news has come to my attention, news that the board must sift through for the long-term security and longevity of Sinclair Pharmaceuticals. As vice-chair, it's my responsibility to expose the concerns even if the timing is awkward."

"Awkward," I repeated. "You called a meeting when you knew that two members of the executive board would not be present. My name is Sinclair. I only have the best interest of this company in mind." I took a breath. "I apologize, I forgot to congratulate you on the marriage of your daughter. I suppose that now makes you a Sinclair by proxy."

"I would say that you missed your chance."

"With Amber? No, Gloria, I passed. You'll both learn that Darius isn't an equal. She didn't just swap one Sinclair for another." I peered across the room, meeting Ella's gaze, and back to Gloria. "I too am married. If it comes to it, be prepared to discuss the addendum."

"Do you have proof?"

"Other than my beautiful bride, yes."

A hush fell over the room as Darius and Amber entered. Mentally, I cringed at the sight of my brother's face. The bruising was more than I'd realized. One eye was practically swollen shut.

"Darius..." Questions came from members of the board and stockholders alike.

What happened?

Are you seriously injured?

Did you file a police report?

Ella was back at my side. In a whisper, she said, "At least he's sticking with the mugging story."

"Oh good," Gloria said, "Art Hatfield is here. Everyone is accounted for." She looked at her watch and spoke to the room, "Ladies and gentlemen, it's about time to call this meeting to order."

A smile curled my lips as Lynwood approached Gloria. As parliamentarian, it was his duty to be certain that our meetings were conducted properly, and we followed *Robert's Rules of Order*. Under normal circumstances, when the chairman was absent, the vice-chair would take charge.

These weren't normal circumstances.

Ella, Dani, and I watched as Lyn Sharp explained

the legal work that transpired yesterday, giving Danielle Sinclair the power as chairwoman. While they kept their voices low, body language suggested that Gloria was caught off guard. Amber walked over to her mother. If she were a cartoon, I imagined smoke coming from her ears.

I whispered to Ella and Dani. "In our game of chess, I believe that is check."

Dani stepped forward. "Ladies and gentlemen, thank you for coming today. I was made aware that our vice-chair, Gloria Wilmott, has a few new matters to discuss with the board. If everyone can take a seat, we'll begin."

"She's good," Ella whispered.

She was. My sister was first and foremost a scientist with her PhD in chemistry. She innately understood the side of Sinclair Pharmaceuticals that I did not. She was as at home in a laboratory as I was in a boardroom, yet when push came to shove, Dani was a Sinclair and as such, could competently navigate the boardroom, much more than I could a laboratory.

The front table filled, with Dani sitting in for the chairman. Gloria took her seat as vice-chair. Rachel Stokes was secretary, Art Hatfield, treasurer, and Lyn Sharp took his seat as parliamentarian.

Danielle gaveled the meeting to order. "Mr.

Sharp, could you please stand and address the board, explaining why I am here in this place of honor."

Lyn stood. "Dr. Sinclair is obviously well-versed in many aspects of Sinclair Pharmaceuticals. As of yesterday, Dr. Sinclair was given the legal power of attorney to speak for her father, Derek Sinclair, and her mother, Marsha Sinclair. Accordingly, she will be conducting our meeting as ad hoc madam chairwoman."

"Thank you, Mr. Sharp," Dani said. "As a matter of order, Mrs. Stokes will read the minutes from our last meeting."

As Rachel Stokes stood and spoke, I watched the uneasiness of Gloria. A quick turn of my head and I saw her displeasure mirrored by her daughter and son-in-law.

"Do we have any reports to share?" Dani asked.

The answer was no.

"Our next item of business is time-sensitive situations."

"Madam chairwoman," Gloria said. "I have a time-sensitive matter to discuss. It's the reason I called this meeting."

"Ms. Wilmott, the floor is yours."

Gloria cleared her throat as she stood. "On a personal note, Dr. Sinclair and both Mr. Sinclairs, the board's thoughts and prayers are with your parents at this difficult time."

My nostrils flared as I inhaled.

Dani was kind enough to acknowledge the comment.

"News of Mr. Derek Sinclair's illness has reached the masses," Gloria went on. "His precarious health status has been reported by social media posts, news agencies, and financial media. Sinclair Pharmaceuticals appears weak in the eyes of the pharmacological world."

"We are not weak," Dani injected before I could stand.

"We are not, but we appear as such," Gloria said. "As a board, we must stand behind the best leader for this company. It is obvious that Derek's children are torn, their attention divided."

Children?

All three of us?

Ella and I exchanged looks of confusion.

"Damien," Dani said, "Mr. Damien Sinclair, you are CEO of Sinclair Pharmaceuticals. Please address the board as to your attention."

Standing, I tugged at my suit coat before stepping away from my seat and walking to the front of the room. After flashing Gloria a smile, I addressed the board as well as the stockholders. "Thank you for your concern, Ms. Wilmott. Our father is on the road to recovery. It's true that my siblings and I have spent many hours in the hospital in Florida. We love our father. That in no way means that Sinclair Pharmaceuticals has been neglected. I am the CEO, and I intend to continue my position. Under my leadership..." I went on to tout the accomplishments and financial gains over the last five years.

"You're still under a probationary period," Gloria said. "One your father felt was necessary to adhere to."

"I am," I admitted.

"Having a probationary CEO does not instill confidence," Gloria said. "I believe it is time for a vote of no confidence."

"Excuse me," I said, "who doesn't have confidence?"

"Me," Darius said, standing.

"And me," Amber added.

Slowly multiple other members of the stockholders stood to their feet. It wasn't close to a majority; nevertheless, it was upsetting.

Dani pounded her gavel. "We just heard from our CEO as to what he has accomplished. I'd like to hear from some of you who want this no-confidence vote as to your reasoning."

Amber raised her hand.

"Ms. Wilmott," Dani said.

"Mrs. Sinclair," Amber corrected.

A din of chatter filled the room.

"Order," Dani said. "Mrs. Sinclair, you have the floor."

"It has come to my husband's attention that his brother, Damien, has and continues to compromise the integrity of Sinclair Pharmaceuticals." Before anyone could comment, she added, "He's working with our competitors."

Chapter 12

Gabriella

Competitors.

Van had been right in his warning. Darius and Amber were working with Dwain Welsh from Moon Medical, gaining access to the pharma coalition, and twisting its objective.

"Mr. Damien Sinclair," Gloria asked, "what say ye to these charges?"

I'd forgotten the antiquated speech during these meetings. If it wasn't so serious for Damien, I'd give more thought to finding myself in a low-rate B-movie with horrible script writing.

Damien spoke to the room. "The accusations are ludicrous. I have not jeopardized Sinclair Pharmaceuticals in any way. Can Mrs. Sinclair" —he was looking at Amber— "be more specific. We have many competitors in our business."

"Moon Medical," Amber said.

The room filled with whispers.

A smile curled my lips as Damien's gaze met mine. He was prepared.

"This coalition isn't new," Damien began. "This board approved our entrance, understanding the benefits..."

This was the Damien I'd tried to forget, the one who commanded a room and a situation. As if a spotlight were shining upon him, as the handsome star of this presentation, he radiated confidence. His words resonated with all who listened. His tone and tenor were entrancing as if creating a magnetizing pull that drew everyone into his orbit.

It took all my willpower not to turn and watch Amber and Darius during Damien's well-articulated rebuttal. My satisfaction came in watching the executive board. Gloria Wilmott for one was taking furious notes as other members of the board nodded their approval. Rachel Stokes was listening. Damien had mentioned that she could be a problem. Not only was she one of the newest appointments to the executive board, but she also shared a close friendship with Amber.

"...I yield the floor, Madam Chairwoman."

The room had returned to silence, the sense of anxiety fading away with Damien's explanation.

Dani turned to Gloria. "This appears to be old business, not time-sensitive."

"Mr. Sinclair," Gloria said, "didn't mention the new arrangement with the coalition, a campaign with a local fraternity—a not-for-profit—that just coincidentally will benefit his new wife. The campaign with Beta Kappa Phi was not approved by our board. We weren't consulted."

"Mr. Sinclair," Dani prompted.

"As CEO, it is within my rights to make business decisions. This is a business decision, agreed upon by Sinclair as well as the other members of the coalition."

My skin felt tight as I stood.

"I yield," Damien said as he turned my direction.

"Mrs. Gabriella Sinclair," Dani said, "would you like to address the board?"

"Yes, Madam Chairwoman."

I began, "Mr. Sinclair brought this campaign to Beta Kappa Phi only one week ago. I think we can all agree that with Derek Sinclair's health issues, Damien had other concerns. That isn't to imply he didn't perform his due diligence for Sinclair. I can attest that he did. Yes, I am still employed by Beta Kappa Phi. As campaign manager, I will be working for all members of the coalition."

Gloria spoke up. "Can we assume that you will be

privy to information from each member of the coalition?"

"Yes."

"Do the members of the coalition know of your marital status? Something Mr. Sinclair was able to fit into his schedule."

Her question caught me off guard.

I hadn't even informed my family of my marital status.

"How is that relevant?" I asked.

"You will have information regarding all the companies within the coalition. I assume you and your husband will share a bed—"

"Objection," Damien said. "What you're insinuating would benefit Sinclair, not be a detriment if it were to occur. However, it will not. My wife is a professional, and as for our wedded status or *sleeping arrangements*" —he emphasized the words— "there will be no effect on the coalition in any way other than an added incentive for the campaign to be successful. That would be for all the companies in the coalition."

I took my seat as Dani banged her gavel. "If this was the smoking gun, Ms. Wilmott..."

"This could reflect poorly on Sinclair if with this new campaign," Gloria said, "other companies grow uncomfortable with the relationship Mr. and Mrs. Sinclair share—"

Dani interrupted. "That is not our concern."

"It is if Sinclair is seen in a less-than-stellar light within the pharmacological community. More than that," Gloria went on, "I'm concerned with Mr. Damien Sinclair's lack of communication with the board of directors. As CEO he must answer to the chair."

"At this moment," Dani said, "that would be me. Damien has communicated with me each step of the way. If the pharma coalition is concerned about their campaign, that is their business, not that of Sinclair Pharmaceuticals."

"As long as he is on probation..." Gloria began.

"Take a no-confidence vote," Darius said, standing and speaking over the growing chatter. He looked around the room. "What shareholders here today were surprised by the low stock revenues the last quarter?"

Heads nodded.

He went on, "Anyone can make up statistics. The real numbers are the ones on our quarterly dividends, and they are obviously down."

"Down," Damien said, "because of reappropriating the funds. Revenue isn't down."

I took in the expressions of the board members.

With each face, I was confident that Damien would survive the vote. I also knew it wouldn't be unanimous, which in itself would be a ding against him.

"Madam Chairwoman," I said, once again standing, "I move that a vote be tabled until I, as the Beta Kappa Phi campaign manager, have the chance to discuss the board's concerns with the other CEOs of the coalition. It seems obvious that the voiced concern isn't about Damien's performance for Sinclair."

"You can't make a motion," Darius said.

Standing taller, I repeated what Damien had told me yesterday. "As Damien's wife, his property is my property. I'm now a shareholder in Sinclair Pharmaceuticals."

"And that is the issue," Amber added. "You can't represent the entire coalition—"

Dani hit the gavel again. "We are not the coalition. I call for a verbal vote to table the no-confidence vote until we have more information making this discussion relevant to our board."

"I second," Lyn Sharp said.

"All of those in favor of tabling the call for a no-confidence vote, say yay."

Responses came from the board and the room.

"Those opposed."

Nays came from the room and front table.

Dani sat taller. "With a show of hands. Yays."

My focus was on the board. Shareholders couldn't vote. Art Hatfield, Lynwood Sharp, and Dani lifted their hands.

"Those opposed."

Gloria, Rachel Stokes, and Grace Haas lifted their hands.

Dani nodded. "The decision is made. The vote will be tabled."

"It was a tie," Gloria said.

It was Lyn who addressed the concern. "Dr. Sinclair has the voting power of both Derek and Marsha Sinclair. That makes the vote four to three in favor of tabling the vote."

"Thank you, Mr. Sharp. Is there any other business?" Dani asked.

"The addendum," Damien said.

Dani nodded. "It was brought to my brother's attention that there is an old addendum in the company bylaws, a clause that would allow the appointment of a CEO if the candidate were married. In essence, it would remove the remainder of Damien's probationary period now that he is married, making him a permanent CEO." She turned to Gloria. "That permanent appointment would demonstrate the strength you are concerned about."

"We can't put someone into a position of power

with a no-confidence vote hanging over his head," Gloria replied.

"I've never seen this addendum," Mr. Hatfield said.

"Me either," Grace Haas added.

Gloria turned to me. "The board would need proof of a marriage."

Dani sat back and lifted her phone. A moment later, she looked up. "The bylaws including the addendum has just been sent to everyone's inbox. I motion we adjourn today's meeting of the Sinclair Pharmaceuticals executive board and plan to reconvene a week from today. During that time, I ask that all board members familiarize themselves with the addendum in question and that Mr. and Mrs. Damien Sinclair contact the pharma coalition and return to our meeting prepared to address the board's concern." She turned to Gloria.

"Second," Gloria said begrudgingly.

Dani hit the gavel. "Meeting adjourned."

Damien came to my side and reached for my hand and spoke low. "This isn't over."

"It should be," I whispered. "You're married."

"We need to make the no-confidence go away." He tilted his head toward the front of the room, where Gloria, Rachel, Darius, and Amber were conversing. "They'd rather take down Sinclair than let me continue as CEO."

Dani appeared at our side. "Mom was right to ask you to keep Darius and Amber away from Dad. I don't know what's with them, but damn."

I reached out and rubbed her arm. "Thanks for the two votes."

Her smile grew. "That was fun." Her expression sobered. "Damien, you don't really think they're a threat, do you?"

"Nice try, sis. We're going through with the bodyguards."

Chapter 13

Gabriella

Johnathon brought Dani, Damien, and me lunch from the second-floor deli to Damien's office. As for my new space, I'd spent about thirty minutes in the office first thing this morning. At that time, the new campaign was far from my mind. However, now as the three of us ate, I was mentally questioning every member of the coalition, wondering if it would make a difference to them that Damien and I were married.

I turned toward Damien. "Shit, we didn't ask anyone to sign an NDA."

His blue stare looked at me filled with puzzlement.

"About our marriage," I explained. "We didn't want it announced."

"You didn't."

"Damien, what about my family?"

He sat taller, inhaled, and exhaled. "Should probably call your parents when we get a chance."

You think?

Moving my chicken salad around in the bowl, I tried to think about our current fires. No doubt, my parents would be a future one, but why add extra flames. There was what Gloria mentioned about the coalition. "I should pass the campaign on to Niles," I said before taking another bite of chicken salad.

Damien shook his head. "I was clear with Mrs. Barns—you or no campaign."

Setting my fork down, I exhaled and leaned back against the chair. "The campaign is a good idea. The coalition has agreed. You can't unilaterally end it." When he didn't respond, I added, "You did that to get me here. I'm here." I lifted my left hand. "We're married. If Gloria wants to use our marriage against the coalition, I don't want to be responsible for the dissolution of what Julia worked to accomplish."

"Losing Moon Medical wouldn't be a significant loss."

"One seventh," I said. "Each member contributes."

"Moon was always my concern," Dani said. "Technically, our propanolol is not a competitor with Moon's anti-anxiety medication. They are two completely different formulas, working on different parts of the brain for different yet similar outcomes."

It had been a while since I'd been in the throes of the pharmacological world. "With Sinclair's formula," I said, trying to remember, "the patient loses the traumatic memories that instigate their fear or anxiety."

"Exactly," Damien said. "The traumatic memories are gone—"

"They are *camouflaged*," Dani said. "Think of memories as files, such as in a computer. The tricky thing is that one memory, be it body or brain, can spark another. It's not as simple as deleting the file. The propanolol is truly groundbreaking in the way it hides the trauma. Those memories are still there, but the formula redirects the brain. It's as if the files are renamed with different pathways."

Damien smiled. "Yeah, that's why you have doctor in front of your name."

"PhD," Dani corrected. She looked at me. "Do you want to know more?"

"Yes," I said, genuinely interested while admitting that this was above my general understanding. "If you can keep it simple."

Wiping her lips with her napkin, Dani readjusted in her chair. "Moon Medical's anti-anxiety formula is a benzodiazepine, a class of depressant drugs commonly prescribed for anxiety disorders, insomnia, and seizures. The benzodiazepines enhance or increase the action of a brain chemical, GABA, by stimulating serotonin and dopamine receptors."

I shook my head. "I'm sorry, that's not simple."

"Their medication basically ups the body's feel-good hormones. Serotonin acts like a hormone. It is also a neurotransmitter, meaning it carries messages between nerves in the brain. Think of it like taking a pill instead of having an orgasm. Yes, you can produce the hormones from physical stimulation. The pill takes out the middleman."

From the corner of my eye, I saw my husband's smirk. "Nice to know," I said, turning to Damien. "Seems you can be easily replaced."

Dani lifted her hand. "Stop. Please. Once I'm getting my share of orgasms, we can revisit this conversation."

"Okay," I replied. "Moon's medication mimics the body's feel-good response to calm a person."

Dani nodded.

"Sinclair's formula eliminates the memory, so anxiety isn't triggered."

"Camouflages it," Dani said. "The memory is still present but hidden." She pressed her lips together. "The propanolol interrupts the sequence of memories, causing a favorable pairing as opposed to a negative one. It's quite remarkable because not everyone has the same trigger. When we were conducting trials, we had military veterans who had different triggers. I remember one man who couldn't watch fireworks. During battle, fireworks are sent up before an offensive. The different colors tell the troops what's going to happen. We had another volunteer who suffered serious injuries in a car accident. Simply getting into a car was torture."

"The formula worked on both of them?" I asked.

"It did. Dosages varied, but that's part of the delivery. We need physicians and psychiatrists to feel comfortable prescribing the propanolol. It's new, and there is always hesitation with what's new. That's why we're still conducting testing. The more data we have, the better."

I nodded. "Moon's product has been around longer."

Damien spoke, "Yes. The physicians, psychiatrists, and facilities are more comfortable with prescribing it. The problem is that their medications flood the system with" —he looked at his sister— "the feel-good hormone. Eventually, it takes more and more to feel good."

"More orgasms," I said.

"Bigger ones," Dani contributed. "What makes your body tingle today won't work in a year or two.

Basically, the one glass of wine that used to calm you takes an entire bottle. This leads to serious side effects."

"What about with propanolol?"

Dani sighed. "There have been a few symptoms similar to those of early-onset dementia. Basically, the medication is camouflaging too many memories. Backing off on the dosage has returned the lost memories, but often with the recurrence of the traumatic ones. Currently, that has occurred in less than 3.2 percent of the cases."

"Is that low?"

"It's higher than we want, but compared to the rate of side effects in psychiatric drugs, it is low."

Damien began to collect our dishes. "As much as I always enjoy my sister's pharmacological lectures, the important thing is that Sinclair and Moon are not in direct competition. The competition occurs at the prescriber level. Do the patients want a treatment plan that includes flooding the body with fake happy juice that will need to continually be increased to maintain efficacy or would the patient benefit from simply masking the trauma and rearranging the memory synapses? At this time, once a therapeutic dosage is established, there isn't need to increase the dose."

I sat back. "Moon isn't the only manufacturer of psychiatric medications."

Damien shook his head. "Hell no. Moon is relatively small in that world. That's why Dwain agreed to join the coalition, for the bargaining power."

My questions kept coming. "Has Sinclair received pushback from other pharmaceutical companies that make psych meds?"

"Lilly has been on the hunt to buy us out."

"They started that before we patented our formula," Dani said.

"Do they make the same kind of meds as Moon?" I asked.

Damien nodded. "It's a growing industry with increased consumer revenue. Lilly, Pfizer, and Forest are the three manufacturers dominating the market."

"How did Julia decide what companies to include in the coalition?" I asked.

"Proximity and size," Damien answered. "Moon is smaller and located in Ohio."

"Sinclair is the only company to market propanolol?" I asked. "Anywhere?"

"There is a small private lab in the Chicago area working on a similar formula." Dani shrugged her shoulders. "The entire operation is shielded. It's difficult to learn too much about it."

I scrunched my nose. "That's odd, isn't it?"

Dani continued, "From what I've learned, the lab is totally funded by endowments. Until they take their formula to the FDA, they can keep it under wraps. There is one..." She let her words fade away.

"One what?" Damien asked.

"I read a paper written years ago by a Dr. Laurel Carlson. It was fantastic. And then she left the university where she worked and last I could find is employed by a large not-for-profit in Chicago. The center's main objective is helping victims of sex trafficking." She sighed. "A population that could definitely benefit from the camouflaging of memories. It's just odd. I can't find where the private lab and the Sparrow Center are connected, but it makes me wonder."

"I recall that name—Carlson," Damien said. "She used to be at a university here in Indy. Things got out of control. I think her partner was killed." He inhaled. "That's another story. For now, are we worried about competition from this Chicago-based lab?"

Dani shook her head. "We're much further ahead in our development, or I think we are."

Damien shook his head. "Fuck, Dani, don't put another damn concern on my plate. It's overflowing."

Dani laid her hands on the table. "Okay, we went down a bunny trail. The point is that if our drug is prescribed, many of the psychiatric drugs become unnecessary. Moon wants to stop us. And according to your friend Van, Dwain Walsh is working with Darius. Why?"

Damien replied, "Shit, at this point, I think they want to burn Sinclair to the ground. We won't let Darius play with our ball, so he wants to take it away from all of us." Damien turned to me. "And no on the Niles thing unless he works with you. I want you close." He looked at his watch. "Speaking of wanting you both close, our three o'clock appointments will be here soon. Did you have a chance to look over the résumés?"

Bodyguards.

"We've been preoccupied," I said. "I'm not fighting you on this. But what are we talking...? Driving with us to work. Being here at Sinclair Corporate. Going out to dinner with us. Sleeping in the next room." I tilted my head. "If it includes all of the above, we need to convince Duchess to move to your house. We'd be too cozy in my condo."

"Let's hear them out."

Chapter 14

Damien

Two women and two men.

I'd read through their qualifications. There was no doubt that they were all competent. It was Leo Conner's advice that I thought about as Ella and Dani spoke to each candidate. As the interviews progressed, I gave Ella's earlier question more thought.

Having Leo's team protecting my parents at the hospital was an easier assignment for the reason that my parents were stationary. Ella and Dani weren't. They were active, social people who were essentially vulnerable twelve to sixteen hours a day.

After the final bodyguard candidate left my office, I turned to the two women I wanted to protect. "Thoughts?"

Dani exhaled and turned to Ella. "I can imagine myself working exceptionally well with Eli."

Ella laughed. "I bet you can."

"Maybe then we can have the orgasm talk."

I lifted my hand. "Whoa. This isn't a dating service." I turned to Ella. "And by the way, you're choosing a woman."

Ella laughed again. "I never remember you being insecure?"

"I'm not."

Dani shook her head. "I'm fried." She stood. "As you know, having a bodyguard isn't my idea. I need to get to my office." She patted my clavicle. "This is your baby, big brother. I could work with any of them. I'll humor you for a time. But if any of them cramp my style, I'm out."

"What style is that...dinner at home, a bath, and falling asleep with your Kindle?"

"Don't knock it."

My sister was right. This togetherness had gone on long enough. "I'll call you."

Ella waited until the office door closed before she stood and brushed the front of her gray slacks. "I should go to my new office. I've barely seen it, and today was supposed to be my first day working on the campaign."

In two strides I was before her, wrapping my arm

around her waist and tugging her soft curves to me. Without provocation, Ella lifted her chin, bringing her luscious lips to mine. In milliseconds the stress of the day faded away into a vapor. Such as a release valve on a pressure cooker, having Ella in my arms calmed my inner turmoil.

"I've wanted to do that since you spoke to the board," I said.

Laying both of her hands on my chest, Ella's sapphire-blue gaze looked up at me.

I ran my thumb over her lower lip. "I can't believe you're really here. Every time I start to think about all the chaos of the last few weeks, I remember that somehow, it brought you back to me." I tipped my forehead to hers. "I don't admit my shortcomings."

Ella laughed. "I didn't know a narcissist could see their own weaknesses."

"Contrary to popular belief, I must not be a narcissist because I'm fully aware that I am incomplete without you. Simply having you here makes me whole. Maybe losing you was exactly the kick in the ass I needed to truly see you."

"I see you, too. You had the room of people riveted as you spoke at the meeting." She shook her head. "I was so proud of you, the way you stood up— your convictions and belief in Sinclair Pharmaceuticals were like a neon sign. I've been trying to think why Darius wanted the no-confidence vote. He can't possibly believe he could step in and do a better job than you."

"He had his chance and he failed."

"Gloria was right about one thing."

I lifted my eyebrows. "What?"

"The members of the coalition should know we're wed. This campaign is a great idea, and I believe in it for Beta Kappa Phi and for the coalition. I meant what I said about not wanting to upset the work Julia's put into creating the unity the seven companies share."

"If Dwain is working with Darius, you won't be the cause of upsetting the coalition."

Ella's eyes opened wide. "My parents."

"I'll call them with you."

"No." She exhaled. "I'll call them. I need to tell them myself."

The complexities of the last week had me overwhelmed. "I should have asked. Are they still in Indiana? We could tell them in person."

"They moved to Arizona about a year ago. Enjoying the retired life."

"I could call Allen—"

Ella shook her head. "We're not flying to Arizona just because we can. We have enough fires burning here, and we both have work we need to do."

My cheeks rose with a grin. "Good. I want you to myself."

"What about the bodyguards?"

"I've decided to have their company evaluate our home security systems, both of ours and Dani's. I've been thinking about hiring all four candidates. They can work out a rotation that works for them and for us. If our homes are secure, their services will only be necessary when we're away from home. That will mean both you and Dani need to communicate with them. No sneaking off to the salon or store without one of them."

"I like that better than having them live with us."

I smiled. "Reading their firearms experience and training had me concerned."

"Why?"

"Because when you scream in the middle of the night, I don't want one of them busting down our bedroom door."

Ella scoffed. "There you go again, being so sure of yourself."

"When it comes to making you scream, yes, Mrs. Sinclair, I am sure of myself."

"What about the coalition?"

"Julia and Van know about our marriage. I told Van on the phone last night. I'll call Julia this after-noon about what came up at the board meeting."

"You told him last night. For the record, you suck at keeping secrets."

I ran my palm over her round ass. "Oh, I can suck a lot more."

She shook her head. "Okay. After I talk to my parents, I'll spend the next few hours organizing what I learned over the weekend. If Julia thinks Niles would be a better choice, I want you to listen to her."

"I'm not letting you work in Carmel." I ran my hands up her back, splaying my fingers and tugging her against me. "I want you here."

"You've got me. Remember, you must let me be me."

She'd said she worried about vanishing.

"You're not disappearing. I promise you."

Ella lifted herself to her tiptoes as she brushed my lips with hers. "I think your idea for the bodyguards will work. I'll see you later."

I didn't want to let her out of my arms, out of my sight. In a matter of days, I'd become completely addicted to Ella's presence. She was a drug. Unlike what we manufactured here, she was the type of drug that revealed memories—memories of our time together—and desire, what we'd shared and what we had in store.

With each hit, I wanted more.

Reluctantly, I released my hold. As she walked

away, I fantasized about removing her silk blouse and stripping her from the long gray slacks.

Ella peered over her shoulder. "Why do I feel like you're looking at me naked?"

A smile broke out across my face. "Apparently, you can read minds."

"Only yours."

Once I was alone, I sat behind my desk and called the security company. The evaluation of our homes would occur tomorrow as would the employment of all four personnel. The person I spoke with offered to start with a month-long contract and we would reevaluate.

A knock on my door caused me to look up.

"Mr. Sinclair," Johnathon said.

There was something odd about his expression. "Is everything all right?"

"Mrs. Sinclair is here to see you."

"Ella doesn't need you to announce her. Let her in."

"No, sir. *Amber* Sinclair."

The muscles of my jaw grew tight as I stood. "I'm busy."

Amber pushed her way past Johnathon and turned to him. "You may leave."

Johnathon's gaze came to me.

"Five minutes," I said, stepping away from my desk.

Once the door closed, Amber smiled. "Only five minutes? Oh, Damien, I remember when you used to last longer."

"Now that you're stuck with an older version, I'd bet you're hoping he can keep it up for five minutes."

Amber sashayed closer, her breasts practically spilling from the V cut of her neckline. "About that."

Lifting my hand, I silently told her to keep her distance. "What the fuck do you want?"

"Darius and I aren't married."

I crossed my arms over my chest. "You lied."

"We didn't lie any more than you and Gabriella did. We had a ceremony. There was a problem with the license."

"What problem?" I asked suspiciously.

"You can only be married to one person, and it seems you and I are still married."

"What the fuck are you talking about?"

Chapter 15

Gabriella

A workman was outside my office door when I arrived.

"Is there a problem?"

"Replacing your nameplate, Mrs. Sinclair."

Fuck you, Damien. Your secret-keeping ability is the worst.

"Hold on to the one that says Crystal, just in case."

"I hope you're joking."

I grinned. "It depends on the time of day."

Opening the door, I went inside. My gaze naturally went to the large window behind my desk, the one that looked out over Indianapolis. I wasn't high up in the skyline; nevertheless, the view was much better than the one I had at Beta Kappa Phi. Sitting behind my desk, I removed my phone from the drawer where I'd left it earlier in the day.

I had numerous missed text messages and calls, three from Niles, one from Millie, and one from my mother.

"Okay, Mom. You're first." I hit the icon, wondering how I would explain the last weekend. As she answered, I decided direct was best. "Hi, Mom. Is Dad around?"

"He's not. He'll be back soon. Is everything all right?"

"I suppose. I thought you should know; I got married this past weekend."

Silence.

Prolonged silence.

"Mom?" I questioned, wondering if our call was disconnected.

"Ella, I think I misunderstood you. You haven't mentioned dating anyone."

"Remember I told you about the campaign that I was roped into?"

"Working with Damien—you married Damien."

I scrunched my nose at the way her volume rose with her statement. "Yep."

"Oh, Ella. Why? What's happening?"

I thought back to the answer I gave Amber in the

hospital. "There's a lot happening, but the real reason I said yes is because" —I took a breath— "I love him." I did. I couldn't deny it any longer. "I care about him. I know I left him, but being back with him feels right."

"Oh, honey. I'm crying."

"Mom, I'm sorry you and Dad weren't there. The wedding was very fast. Damien has offered me a big ceremony in the future. His dad is in the hospital with some heart problems. We'd like to have all four of you and the rest of our family around."

Mom took a deep breath. "That's not why I'm crying. I always thought Damien was special. I also understood why you left. If you feel more confident with him now, Dad and I support you. You're a grown woman. Of course, I'd love to share a ceremony of your union along with the Sinclairs, but that's your decision, dear. We trust you."

A lump formed in my throat.

"Thank you for trusting me."

Mom's voice regained her usual strength. "We trust him too. In many ways, Damien has reminded me of your father. They're complicated men, or that's what they want the world to believe. Men like that need strong women. That's you, Ella. Stay strong."

"Thanks, Mom. Things are very busy right now— a million fires. I'll let you know about a ceremony and when we can get out to Tucson."

"You're always welcome. I'll tell your dad." She paused. "Is Derek going to be okay?"

"We hope so. I'll call back soon. Love you."

"Love you."

Apparently, the cat was out of the bag.

My next text was to Niles. In the last few years, he'd filled the spot of my best friend. If this marriage wasn't going to be a secret, I wanted him to hear it from me.

"Hey, back in Indy. Missing you from this new office. Do you have a minute to talk?"

As I waited for his response, I called Millie Barns's office number. Her secretary put me right through.

"Ella, I was hoping to hear from you before now."

"I'm sorry. I didn't have my phone with all the meetings today."

"It's nearly five on Monday. You met with the pharma coalition over the weekend," she said. "After hearing from Dwain Welsh, I expected you to call first thing after getting back to town."

Well, there's been a lot happening. Instead of saying that, I sat forward, putting my elbows on the desk. "When and what did you hear from Dwain Welsh?"

"He contacted me on Sunday. As you know, Moon Medical has been a Beta Kappa Phi donor for years. He wanted reassurance that even with this new campaign we would continue in that relationship. It seems he is concerned about the coalition—about our representative working from Sinclair Corporate. I have a call out to Mr. Sinclair. He also hasn't returned my call. I'm beginning to think we may have been premature about your move."

I shook my head. "This was discussed in Wisconsin. The members of the coalition want their information in a secure environment. That is what Damien supplied here at Sinclair Corporate."

"It seems that Mr. Welsh is particularly concerned with Mr. Sinclair's access to the information. He mentioned that Mr. Sinclair may be exiting the CEO position."

The hell?

The small hairs on the back of my neck stood to attention—little soldiers ready to do battle for my husband. "He's not."

"Mr. Welsh spoke of a temporary replacement— Mr. Darius Sinclair."

Temporary?

"No," I said more adamantly. "Millie, I know

what's going on. Darius is not taking Damien's position temporarily or permanently. And honestly,
while I might not be the right person to spearhead
this campaign in the eyes of the coalition, that
doesn't mean the campaign should be dead on
arrival."

"I'm concerned that we jumped the gun on this. If
there's already discontentment amongst the coalition
members, Damien Sinclair is guilty of breach of
contract. He promised us the coalition, yet he hasn't
delivered."

Two weeks ago, I would have easily dismissed this
attack on Damien. Now, I was in full attack mode.
"Damien has delivered. We met with the CEOs of
the coalition. Julia Sherman is the chairwoman. We
have her full support. Let me talk to Damien. He is
many things, but he wouldn't purposely mislead us. In
the little time I've put into the campaign, I can see
the possibilities for Beta Kappa Phi and for the
pharma coalition. If the coalition doesn't want me, I
suggest Niles."

"Mr. Walsh didn't say you were the problem. It's
your proximity to Sinclair Pharmaceuticals." She
paused. "Why would the coalition doubt your
ability?"

I inhaled. "It isn't my ability. It's my relationship
with Damien."

"You two have a working history. He was your boss."

For an intelligent, competent woman, Millie was clueless.

Clearing my throat, I spoke, "As of this last weekend, he's my husband."

"Ella, we need to talk."

I rolled my eyes.

"Millie, it's very complicated. Not only did I work for Damien, but the reason I never mentioned my connection was that we had a personal relationship."

"Why didn't you tell me when I suggested this campaign?"

I covered my eyes with one hand and lay back against the chair, my temples beginning to throb. I practically begged her to assign someone else. Nevertheless, I pushed forward, not backward. "The past is insignificant. We're married. I want to continue my work with Beta Kappa Phi. I don't believe marriage is a ground for firing."

"No one is talking about firing you. There is an obvious conflict of interest."

"There isn't," I protested. "I want what's best for Beta Kappa Phi and what's best for Sinclair Pharmaceuticals. The coalition is comprised of non-competing companies that were aligned for the purpose of supporting one another. My work with the campaign will benefit all the companies, yes, including Sinclair."

Millie's voice filled with exasperation. "I need to call legal."

"Don't kill the campaign, Millie. Let Niles spearhead it. I'll take a lesser position."

"The compensation—"

"I don't care."

"Come to my office tomorrow. I'll be here at 8:00 a.m."

Telling her no was on the tip of my tongue. Then again, Millie Barns was still technically my boss. "What can I bring to assure you that this campaign is worth our effort?"

"At this moment, I don't know. Be here tomorrow."

"I will."

The line went dead.

"Shit," I sighed, tipping my head back against the desk chair.

I typed out a text message to Damien.

"Dwain Welsh contacted Millie yesterday."

Next, I opened a text message from Niles.

. . .

"Leaving soon. I'll call on my way home. How was your weekend? All work and...any play?"

I shook my head. He had no idea.

My phone dinged. The message was from Damien.

"On my way to your office. We need to talk and I'm guessing alcohol might be a good addition to this discussion. Let's get out of here. Tomorrow is another day."

I texted back.

"Bodyguard?"

He replied.

"They start tomorrow. Tonight, you're all mine."

. . .

I wasn't sure how he'd done it. Yet looking down at my left hand, I knew that being all his was where I wanted to be. I turned off my computer and retrieved my purse from the desk drawer. It was only a little before five.

Playing hooky was acceptable when you did it with the boss.

Chapter 16

Damien
Over a year ago

I stared up at the ceiling, watching the headlights from the street below chase away the shadows, as various degrees of light and dark danced high above. Turning to my side, I took in the sleeping woman. Her long golden hair fanned behind her head. Her lips were parted. Soft sounds of breathing created a hum.

Our earlier conversation ran on repeat in my head.

Marriage.

Unable to sleep, I exhaled a long, exasperated breath before slowly rolling to the edge of the bed and slipping out from under the blankets. As I searched for my clothes, Amber rolled, her arms searching where I had just been.

"Damien?" She squinted her eyes, searching through the momentary darkness.

"Go to sleep. I'm getting some water."

"Come back to bed as soon as you can."

I nodded, knowing it was a lie. Wearing only my boxers, I once again took her in. A quick glance told me that in only seconds, her eyes were closed, and she was making her way back to dreamland.

Sleep wasn't something I could do.

Running my hand over my hair, I stood for a moment, watching the woman who could be my forever. I didn't feel it.

Am I supposed to?

I was far from a romantic.

Nevertheless, the longer I lay in her bed, the heavier my chest felt. I had to move before I suffocated beneath the growing weight.

Amber Wilmott.

I'd known her most of my life. Her mother had been part of the Sinclair Pharmaceuticals executive board since I was a teenager. Her father was in the US Senate before his passing. Our families were close —dinners, cookouts, even vacations. Jordon Wilmott aided Sinclair with a few government approvals back in the day. Despite my knowing Amber for so long, there was a sense of familiarity that was missing and had been since my last relationship fell apart.

Fucking Ella.

I couldn't think about the void she left.

Gathering my clothes, I made my way down the hall to Amber's kitchen. The clock over the stove said it was only a little before two in the morning. Time to sleep.

My mind was too chaotic to sleep.

This was supposed to be a happy day, euphoric even.

The day I proposed.

I didn't propose. The subject of marriage came up again as it often had since Amber and I began dating. It was time. I was in my late thirties, and not getting any younger. My career was moving the right direction. And then there was the bombshell Gloria dropped on us a few days ago. By marrying, I could fast-track my probationary period as CEO and get the permanent title.

The news had come as such a shock, I called my father.

He said he wasn't aware of the addendum, yet I had a copy of the bylaws and could read it in black and white. After sending him a copy, Dad did what he always does. He added his two cents.

"Don't marry someone for the wrong reason. If you love her, then consider the permanent title the cherry on the top. If you don't like the sundae below, that cherry is fucking insignificant."

His advice was eating at me, nibble by nibble.

Amber could be fun to be around. She enjoyed the spotlight. Fancy dinners and nightclubs were her thing. Tall, blond, and curvy, she looked good on my arm. More than once, her mother had commented on how we would make a power couple.

When it came to sex, she was a wildcat. Nails and teeth and willing for anything.

My mind went to another woman.

She'd left me but only physically.

Ella came to my mind more often than I would like.

While pushing my cock into Amber's asshole as she begged for more, I'd have flashes of the one who never let me do that.

It made no fucking sense.

I craved control, especially in the bedroom, and still my thoughts went to the woman who while fantastic in bed, gave me limits—guardrails, so to speak.

Fully dressed, I sorted through the papers we'd left on Amber's counter.

My stomach dropped as I held up the license.

I remembered earlier in the afternoon.

"Let's do it," Amber said. *"My mom will be ecstatic."*

"*Don't you want a wedding?*" I asked.

"*This is just the license. In Indiana it's good for sixty days. We'll plan a ceremony.*" Her eyes opened wider. "*On the canal. It will be gorgeous.*"

My mind went to my probation. This would end it almost two years early. One less thing to deal with. The excitement on Amber's face was contagious. "*Can you plan a wedding in two months?*"

"*I can do it. After all, Damien Sinclair should have the best and biggest wedding Indianapolis has ever seen. Our pictures will be all over social media and local business journals. The marriage of the century.*"

If yesterday was day one, Amber and I had fifty-nine days to make the license legal. All we needed was the officiant's signature.

I couldn't ignore the sense of doom hanging over me. I was a man who took what he wanted, but I knew that what I wanted or who I wanted wasn't Amber Wilmott.

Pulling out my phone, I hit my sister's number.

"Are you dead? If you're not, call back in the morning."

"Dani."

There must have been something in my voice.

"Are you okay?" She sounded more awake.

"I'm kind of...I thought if I could talk...never mind. Get some sleep."

"Damien," she said, "where are you? Do you need me to come and get you?"

"I was wondering if I could come to you."

"Yes. Of course. Have you been drinking?"

"No, but if you have bourbon, get it out."

After disconnecting the call, I shone the light from my phone on the license. Everything within me wanted to rip it—to tear it in half. However, if I did, I also feared I'd fatally damage my position at Sinclair.

If I didn't tear the paper, maybe Amber and I could work out a truce.

Instead of ripping the license, I crumpled it, and finding another piece of paper, I wrote a note. Yes, it was probably the coward's way, but at least I wasn't ending our relationship via a text or a tweet.

Amber,

> *The license was too much. Too fast.*
> *It's not you. It's me.*
> Okay, that was fucking bullshit.
> *It is me. I need time, more than sixty days.*
> *Have a good life.*
> *D-*

. . .

I left the note with the crumpled license and my key to her apartment on her kitchen counter.

Once outside, I lifted my face to the sky with the sensation that I'd shed a tremendous load. My steps were lighter. The night noises were louder. My inner buzz was stiller.

Amber wasn't my future.

There was no denying that.

Repercussions would undoubtedly come, but no matter what they were, they were better than marrying the wrong person. Fuck, I had the right person. My thoughts went to the diamond ring in my dresser at home. The idea of putting it on Amber's finger made me physically ill. She deserved to marry someone who loved her.

That wasn't me.

The mostly empty streets allowed me to speed from downtown to the north side. By the time I reached Dani's condo, I felt hundreds of pounds lighter. It was closer to one hundred and forty pounds lighter, but lighter, nonetheless.

Dani answered the door wearing pajama shorts and a soft top. "I have bourbon. Talk to me."

"Good news or bad news first."

She closed the door and led me to her kitchen table where she had a bottle of Four Roses and two shot glasses. "Bad." She poured two shots.

As I lifted the glass to my lips, I laughed. It was a full-blown, out-of-control moment, and I was sharing it with one of the only people in my life who I fully trusted.

"You're losing it, Damien," Dani said with a grin.

Pulling out chairs, we both sat, me wearing yesterday's suit minus the jacket and tie, and my sister in her pajamas with her hair piled on her head.

"I don't know which one is the good and which one is the bad."

"How about chronological?" she asked.

"Today, Amber and I went to the county clerk's office."

"What the fuck?" Dani's eyes opened wide. "You're going to marry her?"

"Do you think I should?"

Dani stood and paced back and forth. "I don't..." Her gaze met mine. "I mean, I'm happy for you if you love her. Or is this about that addendum?"

I reached for my sister's hand. "Sit down and have another shot. There's more to the story."

"Okay," she said, nodding and sitting with one leg bent beneath her. "Pour."

I poured each of us a second shot.

Dani lifted hers to her lips. "Give me the other news."

"I crumpled the license, wrote her a Dear John

letter, and left her sleeping in her bed." I shrugged. "Not John, but you get the idea."

"Let me get this straight. You and Amber applied for a marriage license. Did you actually marry?"

Shaking my head, I said, "No. The license is...was good for sixty days. No officiant. We didn't marry."

"And you left her—like broke up?"

I nodded. "That about sums it up." I tilted my head. "Give it to me straight. Am I an asshole?"

"Well, yeah, but that's not news." A smile curled her lips. "If you wanted to marry her, I'd support you because even being an asshole, I love you. Am I happy you changed your mind? In a word, yes." She lifted another shot in the air.

Filling my glass, I lifted mine to hers. "Cheers." The liquid must have completely numbed my throat because as I swallowed, the initial burn was gone. "At this rate, Mom and Dad are never getting grand-children."

"Speak for yourself. I'm five years younger than you."

Placing the glass on the table, I spoke slowly. "Mom and Dad. I kept thinking about them."

"They'll support whatever you decide."

"It's kind of crazy that having happily married parents is infuriating."

Dani laughed. "I get that. I date a guy and think, will I ever be like Mom and Dad?"

"Amber isn't the woman I want to spend my forever with."

"Then it's good you realized now." Dani grinned. "Have you met that woman? I'm not sure I've met the man."

"I think about someone, a lot. Maybe there is someone else."

Dani raised another shot. "To our someone else."

Chapter 17

Gabriella
Present

As Damien drove us north of the city, I took in his profile. While the last week and a half had been a whirlwind or more accurately, a tornado, there was a sense of contentment in where we landed. We'd fallen from the cyclone into one another's arms.

The stress I continued to see etched into the lines on his face drew me to him. The man I'd more than once named the devil was fighting his own demons. I reached across the console and squeezed Damien's thigh. "Have you heard from Marsha?"

His navy gaze came my direction as if my speaking had pulled him from somewhere deep in his thoughts. "She texted earlier. Dad is awake and talking." He scoffed. "Mom said he's irritated—even more than usual."

"That's good...that he's awake."

Damien nodded.

"Did you tell Dani about the bodyguard schedule?"

"Yeah. It may not—"

"You've changed your mind?" I asked.

Damien laid on the horn and spewed a few vulgarities as another car pulled in front of us in a roundabout. Running his hand through his hair, he turned my way. "Fuck, sorry. I'm on edge."

"You have every right to be. This entire mess with the executive board is ridiculous. I'm meeting with Millie in the morning. I'll know more about Beta Kappa Phi's stance on the campaign. Did you talk to Julia?"

"Fuck. No. I can call later."

Once again, I reached across the console. "You're not alone. I'm here. I believe in you. You've never lied to me. You want your dad to be better. You want what's best for Sinclair. We'll get through this together."

As he turned the car onto my street, Damien laid his hand over mine. "I never meant to lie."

My heart skipped a beat. "What do you mean?"

The tendons in his neck pulled taut and his chiseled jaw was rigid.

"Damien."

"We need to talk. I've got a call out to Timothy Evans. He's with Sinclair legal...if you don't remember him. He works with Stephen, who is still in Florida with Dad."

"Is this about the addendum?"

Damien pulled his car into a parking space on the street and shut off the engine. "What kind of alcohol do you have on hand?"

"Mostly wine. I think there's an old bottle of bourbon my dad left after his last visit."

Damien reached for my hand. "I fucking love you, Ella. I have since" —he touched the diamond on my fourth finger— "before I bought this ring."

I lifted my other hand to his scruffy cheek. "I told Mom that when I called. She was shocked that we married, but I told her the truth. I love you. I care about you. I didn't mention that we've agreed to work on our relationship."

"Rekindle."

A smile lifted my cheeks. "Rekindle. When I left you, I concentrated on the negative. How you were a workaholic and how it seemed you cared more about Sinclair than you did me." I placed a finger over his lips as he began to speak. "Damien, that wasn't your fault. Not totally. I see you differently now. You have every right to be concerned about Derek and about the company, even the coalition. I'm not jealous of that. I want to be a part of it, to share your load."

Damien's nostrils flared.

I looked out the side window and back to Damien. "We could go inside."

As I unlocked the front door to the condo, I had a thought. "You need a key."

"And you need one to my place. *Ours*."

Although we'd spent last night here in my condo, I had the sensation as if Damien was visiting, not staying. Stepping inside we were met by our greeting party—Duchess. She ran toward us and rubbed around my ankles before doing the same to Damien.

"You really are the only other person in the world she likes," I said as he picked her up from the floor.

"Hello, Duchess."

The timbre of his deep greeting made me smile.

She responded with a push of her head against his chin.

"I could cook dinner," I offered, wondering what I had in the refrigerator or freezer that I could make into a meal.

Damien draped his suit coat on the back of one of the chairs at the breakfast bar and began rolling the sleeves of his shirt to his elbows. "Let's order delivery."

"I can cook," I said, slipping out of my heels.

His smile formed. "I'm hoping that tonight we'll utilize other skills than your culinary ones."

"Then how about that bourbon or would you like wine?"

"I'll start with wine in case you kick me out."

Why would I do that?

Opening the wine refrigerator, I pulled out a partial bottle of chardonnay. "This?" I looked in the refrigerator. "I have others, and I think there's a cabernet in the cupboard."

"Cab," he said, opening the cupboards.

Taking two wine goblets from the cabinet, I sat them on the counter and handed Damien the wine opener. Once the glasses were filled, we each took one as he led me by my other hand to the living room.

"Why would I kick you out?" I finally asked.

After a hearty sip of his wine, Damien sat back. There was something in his expression I couldn't identify. "Amber came to my office this afternoon."

I set my glass on the table in front of the sofa. "Is this why you've been quiet?"

As he nodded, my stomach twisted.

"Whatever it is, we will make it work."

He closed his eyes and exhaled. "I can't even say it."

"What?"

Standing, Damien paced between the fireplace and the windows that led to my back deck. "It's so fucking unbelievable. I told you I called Timothy."

"I don't understand."

"Amber and I broke up."

I nodded.

Damien returned to the sofa. Sitting, he leaned forward with his hands between his spread knees and stared toward the floor. "She wanted to marry. I knew about the addendum, but I didn't care. I knew she wasn't my *person*, my *one*. You played a recurring role in my dreams. I'm not saying I was waiting for your return; I just knew she wasn't the one."

"Why was she in your office?" There was an edge to my voice.

"She told me that she and Darius weren't married."

I pulled back. "They lied?"

"According to her, they had the ceremony. They applied for the license, like we did. There's no wait in Florida, so it takes time to get the permanent license. Their license hit a snag."

My curiosity was piqued. "A snag? What kind of snag?"

"According to Indiana records, Amber is already married."

A cold chill scattered over my skin. "Married. Married to who?"

His eyes closed and Adam's apple bobbed. "Me."

"What the hell?" I stood, backing away from him. "You're married? I asked you, and you said you didn't marry her. You just said you broke up when she wanted to marry."

Damien was on his feet and coming toward me.

"No." I lifted my hands. "Don't touch me. Explain why you lied."

Oh my God. He lied to me.

I reached for my temples. "I can't believe this. I'm such a fool."

"Ella, you're not a fool. It makes no sense, but I didn't know we were married." He opened his eyes wider. "I'll show you my taxes. I filed single."

"Your taxes. Your taxes." I said the phrase louder each time. "How could you be married and not know you're married? Were you drunk? High? What?"

"Let me explain."

"You can't explain this." I shook my head. "You lied. I asked one thing of you. I asked you not to hurt me."

"Ella, listen to me."

My attention went to my left hand. With tears in

my eyes, I removed the two rings. "Take these and go. I'll tell Millie tomorrow that everything was a mistake. If the coalition still wants a campaign, you'll need someone else." I crossed my arms over my breasts. "Go."

"Fuck no." His volume rose. "I'm not going until I explain what happened."

Sniffing, I reached for my glass of wine and sat on the sofa. "Fine. Explain, then leave."

His head wobbled on his neck. "Fuck," he roared. "I didn't marry her."

"Yet you *are* married."

"Legally, it seems so."

A sob bubbled from my chest.

I'd trusted him. I wanted to help him.

Looking at Damien, a rush of memories returned, ones I'd concentrated on when I left. The negative ones. "You are the devil."

"Fuck, Ella, listen. Over a year ago, Amber and I went to the county clerk's office for a marriage license. Yes, we both went willingly. We didn't marry. We got the license. In Indiana, that license is good for sixty days. I knew it was a mistake. I also knew it would save my place as CEO, but my fucking parents..."

I narrowed my eyes. "What about your parents?"

"They have a good marriage. I've witnessed it all

my life. The night Amber and I got the license, I knew I'd never have that kind of marriage with her. That night, I left her. I left her in her condo with a note. I know that was a shitty way to break up, but I couldn't continue. Leaving that night, I balled up the license and left it with the note and my key to her place. I fucking drove to Dani's place in the middle of the night and told her what I'd done."

"Did you sign the license?" I asked.

"I did, at the clerk's office. There wasn't a ceremony. No official. I should have ripped the damn license to shreds, but I never dreamt that she'd find a way to file it." He lifted his hands to the top of his head and flexed his arms. The seams of his shirt pulled tight over the strain. "She never told me until today."

I closed my eyes, trying to make sense of what made no sense.

"Our marriage isn't legal?"

Damien shook his head. "Amber showed me the email she received from the Florida courthouse where she and Darius said their vows. Their license wasn't approved because—"

"She's already married."

He nodded. "We'll get the same response." His eyes pleaded for me to listen. "Believe me. I didn't know I was married. I don't think it's even legal.

Fuck, it can't be. That's what Timothy said. We'll get it annulled."

Married.

He was married.

I slept with a married man.

"Oh my God, I'm the *other* woman."

Damien crouched down near my knees and looked up at me. "No, Ella. You are the only woman. This is a mistake. That conniving bitch had the license filed under false pretenses."

"She never told you?" I asked.

"She tried to call me a few times, and I blew her off. One of the first times I saw her, after the night I left, was in Florida after Dad's first heart attack."

"How long have you been married?"

"I'm not sure when she filed the license, but I left her about fifteen months ago." He stood. "My taxes—"

"Stop about your taxes." I stood too. "You should not be on probation. You've been married for over a year. She could have gotten you off probation."

"She didn't want to help me. I wouldn't speak to her."

More and more thoughts were coming to my mind. "Why would she marry Darius if she knew it wouldn't be legal?"

"She said she thought I'd be jealous. She never

expected me to return to the hospital with you. With her plan, when I was upset, she'd tell Darius the truth —that she and I were already married. Then the two of us would live happily ever after."

"Is that what she said?"

Damien nodded.

He reached for my hands. "Please, Ella, believe me. I had no idea."

Chapter 18

Damien

"Who knows about this?" she asked.

I shook my head. "I told Timothy the entire story. He's searching for a copy of the license. It's public record. We need to learn who Amber had sign the license and file it."

"Whoever they are, they lied."

"It's definite grounds for an annulment," I said. "I did some quick research after she left my office. An annulment takes about thirty days after it's filed."

Ella's eyes opened wide. "What if she fights it?"

"If she does, she's going to jail for falsifying legal records."

Her nose scrunched. "How did you react? How did she react?"

"I was fucking stunned and angry. She was manipulative and angry." I forced a grin. "Remember what I said about Allen and Angie on the plane, about them hearing more disagreements than agreements?"

Ella nodded. "Angie told me she was glad I was back."

Closing my eyes, I let out a long breath. "Today, in my office, we were loud. Unless someone overheard, no one besides you and Timothy know on my end. She's probably told Darius."

"Oh my God," Ella said, lifting her glass and draining the rest of the wine. "Do you still think he's dangerous?"

"I don't know. If he is, this will only add fuel to the fire." I met her eye to eye. "Do you want me to leave?"

Ella tilted her chin down and ran her hand over her forehead. When she looked up, there were fresh tears in her eyes. "I feel so stupid."

"You're not. I didn't know."

"Who will believe that?"

"I only give a fuck about one person, and I'm looking at her."

Ella looked up. "If I told you to leave, would you?"

"I don't want to."

"Would you?"

My fingers balled into fists at my side. "Ella."

"Would you?" she asked again, louder than before.

"Damn it, I love you. I fucking got you back. I

never should have let you walk out on me in the first place. I don't want to leave. I don't care about a fucking piece of paper. I love you." The rings on the table caught my attention. I lifted the engagement ring. "This is yours. It always has been yours. Will you wear it?" When she didn't reply, I added, "I'll leave. I'm also leaving this ring with you. It belongs to you. This won't be two damn years of separation, Ella. You have my word. I'm going to hound you every second of every day. We're meant to be together. I need you to believe that as much as I do."

My teeth ached under the pressure of my clenched jaw as I waited for Ella to speak, to say anything. She didn't.

"That fucking cunt," I growled. "I'm going to make this right. I promise."

"I need time to think."

Inhaling, I called on all my self-control. "I'll give you time." I handed the engagement ring her way. "Please take this. Even if we're not married, we can be engaged."

Ella reached for the ring. "Tomorrow, I'll tell Millie that I'm stepping down from the campaign."

My fucking heart was being ripped from my chest. "Please don't."

She stood taller. "Please keep me informed about Derek."

"I will. What about my things upstairs?"

Before Ella could answer, her doorbell rang. Duchess came running from the front of the house. When I turned toward Ella, her forehead was furrowed. "Did you call for food?" she asked.

"No. Are you expecting anyone?"

The doorbell rang repeatedly.

"What the fuck?"

We both walked down the hallway toward the foyer. Through the lead-glass sidelight was the distorted image of a person. A man. A tall man.

The small hairs on the back of my neck stood to attention.

I shot out my arm. "Ella, stay back."

The man was now pounding on the door. "I know you're in there. Open the damn door. Your car is right here. I'm not leaving."

Ella's eyes opened wide. "Darius?"

"Fucker."

Ella reached for my arm. "Damien, don't open the door. He sounds nuts. We can call the police."

I wasn't going to hide from my brother behind a door.

The pounding continued.

"I'm going to handle this," I said, going to the front door, turning the bolt, and opening the door. "Shut the fuck up."

"Let me in."

"Leave," I said, "you're making a fool out of yourself."

"You think you can win. You always have. You're nothing but a spoiled asshole who wants everything I've ever had." His volume was getting louder with each phrase.

Opening the door wider, I said, "Fucking get in here and quit making a scene."

"A scene. You think this is a scene?" As Darius's gaze fell on Ella, his volume lowered. "Oh, Gabriella. Has my brother told you that he's a cheating piece of shit? Has he told you about your marriage?"

"Ella knows everything," I answered.

Darius took a step toward her. "Maybe you and I should find comfort in one another."

Ella's arms were crossed over her breasts. "Darius, I think you should go home."

"Home?" he questioned as he looked around Ella's front rooms. "I don't have a home. My wife is married. I've been cut off from my father. And my plan to secure my rightful place in" —his volume tripled— "*my father's company* is going up in fucking smoke." He took another step toward Ella. "But I bet you could make me forget my problems. I'd make you forget yours too."

The actual fuck.

I grabbed Darius's shoulder and spun him toward me. "Leave Ella the fuck alone."

"She's not your wife. Just like Amber isn't mine."

Fisting the front of my brother's shirt, I stepped closer, my warm breath hitting his bruised face. "I beat the shit out of you once, I'll do it again."

"Fucking hit me. This time, I'll have your ass in jail."

Letting go of his shirt, I pushed him away.

Darius stumbled before catching his footing. "I'm the oldest. Dad wanted me to run Sinclair."

My voice was finding its steady volume, timbre, and tone. "He gave you the chance. You failed. That's on you."

"This isn't done." Darius pointed his finger at me. "You don't get to win. Not again. Fucking Marsha will kick me to the curb if Dad dies. I can't land on the curb if I'm Sinclair's CEO."

"You're delirious."

"No, brother," he said. "I'm warning you. I'm taking your position and your wife." He turned toward Ella. "I might even take your mistress, too."

"Fuck you, Darius," Ella said.

The asshole grinned. "Sure, sweetheart, we can work that out."

Fuck the damn police.

Once again, I grabbed his shirt. "Get the fuck out

of here, or I'll gladly sit in a jail cell, knowing you're in the hospital." With my free hand, I opened the front door. "Don't come back." I shoved him to the top step and slammed the door.

As soon as it was closed, Ella came my way. She wrapped her arms around my torso with her body shaking.

"I'm so fucking sorry."

She looked up. "Don't go."

Chapter 19

Gabriella

My body trembled. My nerves were shot. This was the elevator scene at the hotel on steroids.

Damien's arms protectively came around me as Darius's words played on a loop in my mind. I clung tightly to his torso, the sound of his heart beating in my ear. Soothingly, he rubbed a circle on my back.

I looked up. "What if he would have come and you were gone?"

"He's mostly talk."

"Damien," I said, taking a deep breath. "I don't know what's happening. I don't even know which way is up right now. I do need to think. I also know I don't want you to leave."

He lifted my chin. "I never fucking wanted to leave you."

Our lips came together.

My mind screamed that I was kissing a married man.

It was my body and heart that didn't care.

After all, only an hour earlier, I believed myself to be married to Damien.

Our kiss deepened as Damien pulled my blouse from the waist of my slacks, and his warm large hands roamed over my lower back. I pressed closer, wanting the strength of his toned body against mine.

He slowly released me and took a step back. "I want you, Ella. I won't leave you, but I need to know right now if this will go further. If you say no, I'll go upstairs, take an ice-cold shower and jack off before sleeping in one of the spare bedrooms. No matter what, you won't be alone. I'm acquiescing to you—to your decision."

Looking in his eyes, I saw the turbulent indecision churning within. Our future was on a precipice. We could be subject to the whims of the world beyond our control, or we could choose to stay steadfast in the commitment we made to one another.

The world would forever conjure storms. To think otherwise was a fool's dream. It wasn't the wind and rain that mattered, but the way we withstood it. Such as the crops in the country fields, the tall stalks of corn survived the summer storms by bending to the wind and gaining strength from the rain. Brittle trees broke, splintering with their unyielding stance.

I didn't want to break.

We could bend.

I took Damien's hand in mine. "If I'm going to hell for loving a married man, I might as well enjoy the journey." I tilted my head toward the staircase. "Come upstairs with me."

Damien lifted my hand to his lips. "I love you, too."

With his hand in my grasp, I led us up the stairs and to the bedroom we'd shared the night before. Once within, Damien closed the blinds and curtains as I began to unbutton the front of my blouse.

He turned on the lamp on the bedside stand, creating a golden glow of light. "I want to see you, to know you're real." In a few strides, he was before me, his large fingers taking over the task of undoing the buttons before he slid the material from my shoulders.

Goose bumps peppered my flesh as his lips found the sensitive skin where my neck and collarbone met. Distracting me with kisses, Damien unclasped my bra and teased it from my arms. I let out a whimper as his kisses moved lower, sucking and nipping my hardening nipples.

Wrapping my arms around his head, I held him close as his ministrations to my breasts instigated a corresponding twisting of my core. Soon, my slacks too were lost to the bedroom floor, leaving me with only my lace panties.

Damien took my hand and lifted it high. "You're so damn beautiful. Spin."

I did, turning a complete circle as if I were a ballerina in a jewelry box.

When I stopped, Damien reached for my hair tie, gently tugging it, and allowing my hair to cascade down my back. It was my turn to tease free the buttons of his shirt before pushing it from his wide shoulders. I unbuckled his belt as Damien kicked his shoes from his feet.

Once we were both clothed only in our underwear, Damien lifted my chin, setting his navy gaze on me. "What do you want?"

"Make the world go away."

"Your wish," he said as he lifted me, "is my command."

My hands went to his solid shoulders, and I wrapped my legs around his waist. Our lips sought one another's as he carried me from the bedroom into the adjoining bath.

Setting me on the edge of the marble vanity,

Damien went to the shower, turning on the hot spray. "We're going to wash the world away."

My smile beamed as I watched him shed his boxer shorts and carefully monitor the water's temperature. His muscles were well defined, from those in his chest and torso, to the tightness of his ass and strength in his thighs. It was as if I were watching Poseidon monitoring the waters of the seas.

Damien snagged the waistband of my panties. I lifted my behind from the counter as he dragged them down, leaving them with his boxers. Next, he offered me his hand. I placed mine in his as I hopped down to the floor. Together we entered the steamy stall.

Closing my eyes, I allowed the warm spray to rain down on me.

The act was cathartic as my hair dampened and my skin covered with water.

Damien was next, stepping under the shower. The way he closed his eyes made me wonder if he was thinking the same as I was, how nice it would be to simply wash away the world beyond our bubble. It was as his eyes opened that I saw the gleam I loved and do love.

It was that look that said he only saw me.

A predatory attraction as if he had me in his snare.

My heart beat faster as he closed the small space between us. Once again, with his hands under my ass, he lifted me. My breasts flattened against his hard pecs, and my core rubbed over his tight abs.

I let out a sigh as he spread my lower lips, and a long finger found its way inside me. I leaned back toward the tile, my eyes on his. Our intense stare-down continued as he added a second digit. I sucked in a breath at the invasion.

"Ride my fingers, beautiful."

My lips quirked. "I'd rather ride your cock."

"You have to earn my cock, Ella. Ride my fingers."

Earn.

It was a challenge I'd willingly take.

Lifting myself higher, I pushed off his shoulders and lowered myself. All the while, we continued our stare-down. Over and over, I lifted and lowered. His fingers stretched and teased. It was as he added his thumb and small circles over my clit that I took a shuddering breath.

"That's it. I want to watch you come."

I wanted the same.

Faster and faster.

I was almost there.

The orgasm hit with a warning tremor before my entire body convulsed and my pussy spasmed around his fingers. For longer than I knew, I rode out the

intense sensation, my lips open and my nails threatening his skin.

When I lifted my head, meeting his gaze, I
grinned. "I don't want the pill equivalent. You're irre-
placeable."

"Oh, beautiful. We're not done. It would take a
whole fucking bottle." His smile grew. "Can you
stand?"

"Stand." I looked around the shower. "I think I
can."

"Good." He lowered my feet to the shower floor.
"Turn around and hold onto the wall."

There was no trepidation or second thoughts.

Damien was directing my pleasure and washing
away the world. I was his puppet to instruct and
manipulate. Putty in his hands, his capable hands. I
widened my stance and placed each hand against the
tile. My splayed fingers were all I saw as Damien's
touch covered me, such as the shower's spray.
Starting at my sides, he moved lower. My torso. My
waist. My hips. My thighs. His touch shifted, inside
my thighs, down to my ankles. He spread my legs
farther apart and back to my ass, he pulled it
toward him.

It was all a prelude, the building of the melody.
The notes that signaled a verse was about to begin.
There weren't words, only notes. Notes that sang

their own introduction. The music slowed, a ritar-dando. The anticipation built. Allegro.

My back arched as Damien filled me, sliding deep within my wet core and stretching me.

The tempo increased.

Vivace.

Presto.

Thrust after thrust.

Damien set the rhythm of the chorus.

My fingers curled as the tension built.

The accelerando wasn't in my mind alone. Damien, too, was moving faster. His breaths panted in my ear. His grip of my hips intensified. All the while, the warm water coated us, washing away our sins until the stall echoed with Damien's roar. His cock pulsated as he filled me. Simultaneously, my core imploded.

Synapse after synapse ignited, radiating through my nervous system until my toes curled and my scalp tingled. My forehead fell against the tile as Damien snaked his arm around my waist, saving me from falling.

"You're mine, Ella," he declared, his lips near my ear. "Mine."

Hating myself for breaking our connection, I spun until we were face-to-face. I recalled my mother's advice.

It takes strong women to love strong men.

I brushed his lips with mine. "And you're mine, Damien. Make it happen. You promised me to rekindle. I'm holding you to it."

"We're stopping Amber and Darius."

I nodded. "*We* are."

Chapter 20

Gabriella

A new day.

New battles.

Damien woke me with kisses over my shoulder and arm as his erection probed my lower back. Last night, he'd done as I'd asked and made the world go away. If only for a momentary time, we relished the bubble of our own making.

Shower sex was followed by dinner, delivered from a local restaurant, eaten naked in bed with our respective bottles of wine. There was brutal honesty spoken as we ate. I learned more about Amber. Nothing made me like her.

Of course, I could choose to not believe Damien about their marriage.

It was that I did believe him.

I'd watched and listened to this man speak in personal meetings, small groups, and to large auditoriums. Damien was a man who set goals and achieved them. In the depths of his being, he believed in the future of Sinclair Pharmaceuticals. I'd seen the tears he tried to hide when facing the reality of his father's ill health. I'd witnessed his wrath when he confronted Darius in the hospital. Those were emotions I'd experienced recently and in our past.

When it came to business, he could be ruthless, cutthroat, and abrupt.

The one thing I'd never witnessed in Damien Sinclair was untruthfulness.

He could answer that everything was fine when it wasn't. He'd claimed that late hours and long days didn't exhaust him when in fact they did. Once I recalled him pretending to like a dessert my mother made—in his defense, it was terrible.

Those were not lies.

Those weren't even untruths.

They were placations.

Words said to ease the burden on someone else.

When it came to things that mattered to Damien, he could be brutally honest.

That was why as we dined on sushi and wine, I made the decision to trust the man I'd fallen for a second time. A marriage license was filed, unbe-knownst to him, with his signature—of which he admitted signing.

After the take-out containers were thrown away, our lovemaking was less about making the world go away and more about making our world stronger. Intimate touches and caresses occurred as we explored one another's bodies. Kisses and licks sent goose bumps over our flesh. The vigor and urgency of our shower sex was replaced by savored encounters, slow and steady. We were both in need of what only the other could provide.

As one of us would nod off to sleep, the one still awake would rouse the other, needing to know that we were still here for each other.

With dawn awaking beyond the blinds, I rolled to face Damien. Bringing my hand to his scruffy cheek, I saw the engagement ring I'd agreed to wear. My gaze met his. "Good morning."

His deep baritone timbre reverberated through me. "Good morning." He tipped his forehead to mine as his hands roamed my body beneath the blankets. "I'll make this right."

"We're right. Us, here." I sighed. "Why can't life be simple?"

He grinned. "If it were, you and I would be

married, living in the house I bought for us, with one or two little Sinclairs."

A giggle came from my throat. "Oh, you think one or two little Sinclairs would be simple?"

"If they're like their mother they would be."

"I'm simple?"

"No, you're very complex." He rolled to his back, bringing me with him until I straddled his torso. Stretching his neck, he caught one nipple and sucked before doing the same to the second. "You're also perfect in every way." He splayed his fingers on my hips and lifted me.

I was the one who directed his now-erect penis.

My eyes closed as I slid down, feeling the stretch. With my hands on his shoulders, I bent my knees, moving up and down. It was as I opened my eyes that I became lost in the kaleidoscope of his orbs. Different shades of blue swirled within, pulling me into Damien's orbit, a magnetic attraction I couldn't break if I wanted to.

All at once, we switched positions—my head on the pillow and Damien above.

"I thought I was perfect," I said with a grin.

"The perfect torture." He kissed my nose. Pushing my knees back, Damien increased his speed. The friction was fantastic as my insides grew tight and my back arched. I held tight to his shoulders as I teetered on the brink of my orgasm.

Gasping for breath, my nerves exploded, setting off electrical charges throughout my body. The tendons in Damien's neck stretched as he too found his release. Our hearts beat against one another's as we steadied our breath and our heart rates returned to normal.

It was after our showers as I was dressing that Damien asked me about my meeting with Millie.

I looked at the clock. "It's in an hour."

"I hate not being with you. But I need to get to Sinclair Corporate."

"Beta Kappa Phi is close. It's why I bought this condo."

"The bodyguards are starting today," he said, looking at his phone. "I'll text for one of them to drive you to your meeting and back to Corporate."

Tilting my head, I sighed. "I was all right with the bodyguard thing in principle, but in reality..."

"In reality, Darius was here last night saying disgusting things. And Amber is a hot mess. We're not taking any chances."

"Fine," I said. "I get the feeling there's no arguing the point."

"None," he replied, knotting his tie.

I took a moment, as he donned his gray suit coat, to admire his reflection in the mirror beside mine. His navy stare met mine as his lips curled. "I like starting our day together."

Nodding, I smiled. "I do too." I turned toward him and took a step closer. Lifting my chin, I brushed his lips with mine. "And ending it. Will you drive me home or will one of the bodyguards?"

Damien wrapped his arm around my waist, tugging me closer. "You'll have me."

"My favorite."

Damien picked up his phone from the vanity and read a text message.

"It seems Deidra will be picking you up in twenty minutes."

"I wanted Eli."

"Oh, sweetheart, you're not getting Eli." He gave me another chaste kiss. "I'll see you at Corporate. Text me when you're with Deidra and when you're headed downtown."

"That didn't seem like an ask."

He shook his head. "It wasn't. Don't poke the bear. Give me the sanity that comes with knowing you're safe."

After Damien left, I collected my things for the meeting with Millie. Mostly, I had my notes and the information I'd gathered on the coalition.

I was almost ready when the doorbell rang.

"This is my driver," I said to Duchess. "Fancy."

Opening the front door, I was met with a green stare, and not from the woman we'd interviewed. "Amber. Why are you here?"

"You're sleeping with my husband. I think we need to talk."

Still holding the door, I didn't budge. "Your marriage isn't legal. You know that."

She scanned the solid door. "Don't you see. You can help Damien get the permanent CEO position by accepting that he's married."

Before I could respond, another car pulled to the curb and a woman in a simple black suit emerged from the driver's seat.

"If you'll excuse me," I said to Amber, "my car is here."

"What do you think the board will say when they learn about Damien's and my marriage? They'll know you're with a married man."

I pressed my lips together. "Will that be before or after they're told about your marriage to Darius, when you knew you were already married?"

"Mrs. Sinclair," Deidra said from the sidewalk.

"Yes," Amber and I said in unison.

"Are you ready?"

"Yes, Ms. Wilmott was just leaving." I reached

inside for my bags before closing and locking the front door.

As I was walking to the car, Amber said, "I'm not giving up."

Chapter 21

Damien

Hitting the button on the steering wheel, I listened to Ella's text message.

"Following your orders, I'm texting my whereabouts. I'm with Deidra. On our way to Beta Kappa Phi. Oh, and after you left, I had a visitor. Your wife."

My knuckles blanched as I tightened the grip of the steering wheel. "Call Ella," I said aloud.

"Good morning," Ella said as she answered.

"I wish we were back in bed saying the same thing."

"Yes, Deidra is here. We're almost to the fraternity."

Hearing her voice made me smile. "Is that your way of telling me to watch what I say."

"I mean, you're not on speaker, but your voice carries."

"What did Amber want?"

Ella hummed. "She wanted to talk about our similar taste in men. Fortunately, Deidra arrived and cut our conversation short."

"Don't fight the bodyguards. She's already come in handy."

"I'm not fighting. I'll call after my meeting."

"Ella."

"Yes," she replied.

"The campaign is important to me but not as important as you. I love you."

"I love you too. Bye." The line disconnected.

What a fucking mess.

"Call Julia Sherman," I said to the car.

"Calling Julia Sherman."

"Damien."

The noise in the background made me smile. "Julia, sorry to bother you. It sounds like you're busy."

"This is just my every day. Do you want to speak to Van?"

"It's you I'd like to speak with. Dwain..."

Our conversation didn't last long. I knew I'd missed a call from Millie Barns, but I believed, given the recent circumstances, Julia would be a better spokesperson for the coalition than I would be.

After fighting stop-and-go traffic off the ramp, I made my way to the garage at Sinclair Corporate. Johnathon's car was already in his space. Ella's assigned parking spot was empty. If I had my way, it would remain that way. The idea of sharing a ride made me grin. Even if her news about a visitor didn't.

"Good morning, Mr. Sinclair," Edgar said at the security stand by the elevators.

"Good morning, Edgar."

"Sure is nice seeing Ms. Crystal around here again."

I wanted to correct him and say Mrs. Sinclair. However, there was a good chance we'd hear today that our marriage license didn't pass muster. And until I got rid of the first Mrs. Sinclair, I couldn't have another.

"I agree," I replied before stepping into the elevator.

Despite the early hour, the top floor was bustling. The receptionists waved as they spoke into their headsets, directing calls. Once inside the maze of hallways, I took the most direct route to my office.

As I entered the front office, Johnathon greeted me with a cup of coffee in his hand.

"Here you are, Mr. Sinclair."

Tilting my head, I bid him to follow me to my office.

Setting my satchel on a chair, I turned and took the warm mug of coffee. "Thank you. Have you heard from Timothy from legal?"

"Yes, sir. He called about a quarter to eight. He said you can call him back, or he'd be happy to come to your office."

"What's my schedule?"

As Johnathon rattled off the day's itinerary, it seemed I had an available slot for Timothy. "Have him come right up. This matter is urgent."

"Sir, I was wondering about the new nameplate outside Mrs.... Ms. Crystal's office."

"Fuck," I growled under my breath.

"If you'd rather—" Johnathon tried.

"No. Have the Crystal nameplate reinstalled." I took the mug of coffee to my desk, and before I sat, I met Johnathon's gaze. "Tell them to keep Sinclair. This is just a momentary setback."

"Hey," my sister called from the doorway. "Did I catch you with a minute?"

She looked rested, which was more than I could say for myself. Between a marathon sex session and worrying about...everything, I didn't get a great night's sleep. "Come in." I turned to Johnathon. "Let me know as soon as Timothy arrives."

"Yes, sir. Coffee, Dr. Sinclair?"

"I'm good. Thank you."

After Johnathon left, Dani closed the door. "I spoke to Mom. They're moving Dad to a less critical room."

"That's the best news I've heard in a minute."

She came closer, taking a seat opposite my desk. "Ella called me last night. I missed her call, and she didn't leave a message. Is everything okay in paradise?"

"Fuck, it's not."

"What did you do?"

I scoffed. "I fucked up but not intentionally. Do you remember the night I broke things off with Amber?"

"Other than it ruining my sleep, it was a great night."

Dani's eyes widened as I told her the new information. The license I crumpled was filed. Legally, Amber and I are married.

"For how long? And she never said a word?"

"Timothy went on a search for the license. I have no idea when she filed. As for telling me, not until yesterday when she informed me that her marriage to Darius is void because she's already married."

Dani shook her head. "That bitch is fucked up. Wait, what do you think this will mean for next week's board meeting?"

"For one thing, I've been married for over a year."

"The addendum."

I nodded. "Darius showed up at Ella's place last night. He's pissed about not being married to Amber. He probably realizes she never intended to marry him in the first place. She said she did it to make me jealous."

My sister laughed. "Oh, I can tell you're green with envy."

"I'm green, but it's not with envy for anything in Darius's life."

"Gabriella is your someone else. I see the way you change when you're with her. I don't mean change. I mean...mellow. She evens you."

"I think I've known ever since she got away that she was my someone. I'm sure as hell not letting this mess with Amber fuck it up."

"Is Ella here?"

I shook my head. "She's at Beta Kappa Phi. The executive director is concerned about the new campaign. It seems that Dwain contacted her." I leaned back against my chair. "Do you ever wish life was simple?"

"You mean like not having a bodyguard drive me to work?"

"How did that go?"

"Well, I'm here." She lifted her eyebrows. "Silas isn't much in the conversation department, but damn, the way his muscles bulge under his shirt was entertaining."

"If I said something to you about the way a woman looked, you'd tell me it was inappropriate."

"It would be. Men are sexist."

I rolled my eyes. "Women aren't?"

She shook her head. "Nope. That's just the way it works."

"Mr. Sinclair," Johnathon said as he opened the door. "Mr. Evans is here."

"Good luck," Dani said, standing.

I stood too. "Thanks, sis. I know Ella believes me. I hate putting her through this. If you get the chance to give her your memories of that night, I'd appreciate it."

"Amber may have helped you."

Pressing my lips together, I tilted my head.

"You've been married for over a year. The addendum states marriage. It doesn't say a word about divorced."

"Annulled," Timothy said as he entered. "You have grounds."

Dani lifted her hands. "I'll leave this to you two."

Dani closed the door as she left, leaving Timothy and I alone. Taking my mug of coffee, I led us to the conference table. "Am I really married?"

"Congratulations are overdue." A fit tall man with graying hair, Timothy was the epitome of an attorney. His words were measured and weighed.

"Shit," I mumbled as we both took our seats. "When?"

"The license was issued in April of last year."

I nodded. "That would be about right."

"The marriage was officiated June third of last year."

"Fuck, it's about our anniversary." I had a thought. "Is there a time constraint on annulments? Do we have to work fast?"

"Marriages of any length can be annulled if they meet the criteria."

"How about I didn't fucking know about it?"

Timothy smiled. "Marriage by fraud and marriage by coercion are both plausible grounds. We can go ahead and file for the annulment, or you can take this further."

"What do you mean?"

He pointed to a signature on the license. "I checked out this officiant."

I leaned forward, reading the name. "Donald Vallencia. Should I know that name?"

"Mr. Vallencia obtained an online certificate of clergy. That is public record. It took a little longer to learn that Mr. Vallencia is Gloria Wilmott's gardener who happens to be in the United States on an O-1 visa. That visa was set to expire last July."

"O-1, what is that?"

"It's a visa for individuals who possess extraordinary ability in sciences, arts, education, business, or athletics."

"Gloria's gardener? Am I missing something?"

"As an employee of Mrs. Wilmott, she was able to file his application for extension. Mr. Vallencia is also a doctoral student for music at Indiana University. He's said to have a tremendous gift, playing multiple instruments. The member of the citizenship and immigration services who ultimately approved the extension clerked for Jordon Wilmott years ago.

"After your marriage license was filed, Mr. Vallencia received a one-time bonus of $100,000 from Gloria Wilmott."

"Fuck," I said, leaning back in the chair. "Don't tell me—Gloria was one of the witnesses?"

Timothy shook his head. "Witnesses aren't required in Indiana."

"I've been married for almost a year. Gloria knew it and Amber knew it, and they sat on it. I could be out of my probationary period. Dad could have avoided the stress with me and the board."

Timothy tapped the papers. "You've got a lawsuit here. Fraud and coercion."

Chapter 22

Gabriella

"*D*o you want me to go into the building with you?" Deidra asked.

I looked at the building where I'd worked for the last two-plus years. "I'm good on my own. Should I call or text you when I'm ready to leave?" I shook my head. "This is new and a bit odd."

Deidra smiled. "Your husband is obviously concerned. In my line of work, if someone is concerned, there's a reason. Text is fine. You have my number."

My husband.

I didn't have it in me to correct her. I was saving up my energy for the discussion with Millie. "I do," I said, getting out of the car.

"Ella," Niles called from a few rows away in the parking lot.

I waited for him to get to me.

"A driver? What is happening? You didn't pick up last night."

"Oh, it's a bit unbelievable. Sorry about last night. There was a major catastrophe."

"A major one," he replied. "I need all the details."

I lifted my left hand. "I'm engaged."

Niles stopped walking and reached for my hand. Slowly, he looked up at me, squinting his eyes and studying my face. "You're still here."

A smile lifted my cheeks. "Thanks for checking."

"Mr. Handsome?"

I nodded. "Yes, there's a bit more to the story, but Millie is waiting for me."

"I can't wait to hear how a weekend business trip turned into a proposal."

A weekend trip.

It felt more like six months.

"I'll fill you in. By the way, you may be getting the coalition campaign. If you do, I'll fill you in on everything."

The doors to the elevator opened and we stepped in.

Niles reached for my arm. "What's happening? Why are you giving up the campaign?"

"I'm not," I said softly as more people joined us. "I'm fighting for it, and the best way to proceed may be without me—at least without me as the campaign manager."

Niles shook his head as the doors opened. "Come to my office after your meeting."

"I will."

Securing the strap of my satchel, I took a deep breath and headed toward Millie's office. With each step, I considered what I had in store and how I'd explain the debacle of my marriage announcement.

It was the beginning of the workday, and friendly faces were hurrying from here to there. I was greeted by welcoming smiles and familiar addresses.

"Ella, what are you doing here?" Rosemary asked, coming to a stop.

"I'm here to see Millie."

She lifted her hand to her chest. "I was afraid she called you about me. It wasn't about me, was it?"

"No, I'm sure you're doing great."

"I haven't been at it long," she said, "but I'm doing my best."

After we said goodbyes, I thought how odd it was that Rosemary considered the time frame not that long, when I was sure I hadn't been in these halls for weeks or months. "Hi, Pam," I said to Millie's secretary.

"Ella, Millie is on a call. As soon as she's off, she'll be ready to see you."

"Okay." I looked around, spotting two chairs next to one wall. "I'll wait for her."

Pam nodded.

I pulled my notebook from my bag, the one with the notes from the weekend in Ashland and about the coalition. Each entry refreshed my memory. The names of the companies and the CEOs. Next was the list of the main revenue sources and their budgets. I was deep down the rabbit hole when Pam called my name.

"Ella, Millie's ready."

"Thank you," I said, gathering my notes and standing. The few steps to Millie's door were as if I were walking through quicksand. I couldn't pinpoint my trepidation, but it was present.

"Hi," I said, spotting Millie behind her desk.

"Please, Ella, have a seat."

Taking a deep breath, I took the same seat I had when Millie railroaded me into the campaign; now I was here to argue that same campaign's worth.

"Congratulations," she said.

Okay, we're going to start with this.

I lifted my left hand. "I spoke too soon. Damien and I are engaged."

Millie opened her eyes wide and pursed her lips. "The two of you didn't marry?"

"We did." I sat taller. "We married in Florida.

We've now been made aware that there's an issue with our marriage license." I shrugged. "Therefore, we're back to engaged."

"Ella, this spontaneous, irrational behavior isn't like you. Is there more to this story?"

"There is a lot more. However, I don't see how any of it is pertinent to my position with Beta Kappa Phi or as campaign manager for the campaign you basically forced upon me."

"I didn't force you." She shuffled papers on her desk. "I believe your behavior is relevant. As a representative of Beta Kappa Phi, your integrity could be in question."

Perhaps it was the lack of sleep. Maybe it was the entire world crashing down, but I wasn't in the mood for a lecture on my integrity.

"Millie, my integrity is not in question. I've known Damien for years."

"You don't just marry someone—"

I lifted my hand. "Millie, if you're talking to me as a friend, I will tell you I appreciate your candor, but you are uninformed. You don't possibly have enough knowledge to pass judgment." Her lips pursed. I went on, "If you're speaking to me as my boss, I believe you're crossing the line. What I do in my personal life is not up for debate. Give it to me straight: are you killing the campaign?"

Millie sat taller. "I've been in contact with our legal department. While they understand that whom you marry or are engaged to is your business, they would like a statement from the coalition that there is still confidence in your ability to act for all the companies."

"I'll get a statement."

She shook her head. "That isn't necessary."

"You just said..."

"Julia Sherman called me this morning."

I let out a breath.

Millie went on, "She has faith in you and your abilities. She also corroborated the information you gave me last night. The coalition agreed with you working at Sinclair Corporate for the reason you mentioned. She stated that the coalition has upheld Mr. Sinclair's promise of working with Beta Kappa Phi."

"You're not killing the campaign."

"I'm not. I'm concerned about Dwain Welsh. Despite what Mrs. Sherman said, he wasn't happy."

"Did you tell her that?" I asked.

Millie nodded. "She said she would take care of it."

"I'm willing to step down and give the manager position to someone competent. I recommend Niles. I believe that the coalition will still require the representatives to work from Sinclair Corporate." I shook my head. "Whomever is doing this campaign will have access to a slew of confidential information."

"Mrs. Sherman wants you, Ella." She paused. "I'm not forcing you. If you felt that way before, I apologize. It was my enthusiasm for the campaign that had me blinded. Do you want to maintain the campaign?"

"I do," I replied, remembering what Damien had said on the phone. He'd said that the campaign was important, but not as important as me. "I believe I can make this work, for Beta Kappa Phi and for the coalition."

"You're walking a tightrope, Ella. If Dwain Welsh or any other CEO feels you've given preferential treatment to Sinclair or unwittingly shared with Mr. Sinclair, Beta Kappa Phi's reputation is on the line."

"Are you saying you don't want me as manager?"

"No. I'm telling you to be careful. Maybe if Damien is replaced by his brother, it will be easier."

I shook my head. "Nothing about Darius running Sinclair Pharmaceuticals would be easier. Damien has shown his competency over the last four and a half years."

"I heard their father has taken ill."

"As I said, there is a lot happening."

Millie took a deep breath. "Tell me what you learned over the weekend."

What I learned.

About the coalition.

Taking my notebook from my satchel, I gave her the structure of the coalition. By the time I left her office, I had Millie's cautionary stamp of approval to keep working the campaign. As I gave that some thought, I decided it was similar to Damien's probationary period. Millie was either giving me the chance to prove myself or enough rope to hang myself.

The jury was out.

Before texting Deidra, I stopped by Niles's office.

After giving me a hug, he closed the door. "What in the world is going on?"

I scoffed. "Too much to say right now. Let me try with the abbreviated version."

Chapter 23

Damien

"Ms. Crystal is here," Johnathon said, speaking through our intercom.

Before I could remind him that she didn't need to be announced or tell him to send her in, the door to my office opened. Pushing back on my desk chair, I scanned from Ella's beautiful hair to her shiny shoes, pausing on all the curves in between.

"You're doing it again," she said, coming around my desk and leaning down for a kiss.

After our kiss, I reached for her shoulders. "Don't stand up. I like the view of your gorgeous breasts."

"Inappropriate." Despite my command, she stood and leaned her round ass against my desk.

"What am I doing?"

"Looking at me as if I'm not wearing clothes."

I chuckled. "I'm seeing the clothes and imagining

them falling to the floor." Standing, I leaned close and whispered in her ear, purposely blowing warm air onto her slender neck. "Did you lock the door?"

"No."

"It's a shame." I ran my hands down her arms with a ghostly touch, watching her reaction. The way the small hairs stood to attention and how her grip of the desk's edge tightened. My words came out breathy. "I guess I can't bend you over this desk, flip up that sexy skirt, and bury myself deep inside your wet pussy."

Ella's cheeks filled with a rosy hue. "How do you know I'm wet?"

"Because I can smell you. And you smell sensational." I leaned back, scanning the front of her blouse. "And your nipples are hard. They're giving you away."

She crossed her arms over her breasts. "Maybe I'm cold."

"Are you...cold?"

"No," she said with a grin as she lifted her arms to my shoulders. "I need to do work today, but I wanted to thank you."

"Lock the door and you can thank me properly."

Ella shook her head. "This is me thanking you."

Falling back into my chair, I sighed. "I'd prefer a blow job."

More shaking of her head.

"What did I do?" I asked.

"You spoke with Julia."

"I did."

"She called Millie," Ella said. "And the campaign is still a go. I offered to step down as campaign manager."

Furrowing my brow, I pressed my lips together.

Ella went on, "Millie said she wants me to continue as we are."

I reached for her left hand. "Even though we're engaged."

Ella nodded. "She wants me to keep the entire coalition happy with the fraternity. No preferential treatment."

"Does having you naked under my desk for an early-afternoon blow job qualify as preferential treatment?"

The color in her cheeks was creeping down her neck. "Since I'm supposed to be working for Beta Kappa Phi, I think the answer is yes. What did you learn from Timothy Evans?"

I inhaled. "Gloria was in on it. The presiding officiant happens to have been her gardener, a talented man from Colombia who took an online test to become a clergy."

"You were married by a gardener?"

"He gardens for money. He's also a music prodigy

—maybe, I don't know. He's working on his doctorate at IU in music. I've heard it's not easy to be accepted into the program. The assumption is that he needed help staying in the US and money. Gloria stepped in and quid pro quo."

Ella shook her head. "A gardener-slash-music prodigy and a hospital chaplain. Planning our wedding is getting more difficult. It will be hard to beat your track record of marriages."

Reaching for her hand, I closed my eyes and sighed. Opening them, I smiled. "Thank you for believing me, and for even joking about this fucking mess." I lifted her knuckles to my lips. "For being here now."

"Maybe I should be the one getting oral."

I patted the desk. "Anytime, anyplace." When she didn't abide, I continued, "Seriously, Timothy says I have grounds for an annulment as well as a lawsuit."

"Because suing Gloria Wilmott and her daughter will be so helpful when the executive board reconvenes."

"She should be removed from the board," I said.

"That's it, Damien. She should be removed. Or she could resign if you promise not to sue, not to make this mess public."

I sat straighter, thinking about Ella's suggestion.

Ella went on, "What they did to you was illegal

and immoral. If they want their actions public, then don't resign."

"I think I love you for more than your forgiving spirit and sexy body."

Ella grinned.

"I love your devious ways, too."

"Talk to Timothy. I don't consider it devious. Showing up at my door as soon as you left, that's devious. Take her down."

"I'm getting hard."

Ella's laugh rang throughout my office. "I'm going to do some work. By the way, Deidra is nice. She sat near Niles and I during lunch. You know, there but not intrusive."

"How is Niles?"

"He's good. Oh, and he thinks I'm crazy, but that seems to be the general consensus. I'm beginning to think it's a requirement for being with you."

"That's why we're perfect together."

"I'm not looking forward to my call with my mom, sharing the change in plans."

"I can tell you I'm sorry again."

Ella laid her finger over my lips. "Maybe it's good. Mom can plan a wedding."

"Let me know how it goes." After Ella offered me a chaste kiss, I said, "We'll drive home together."

"Come to my office when you're ready to leave."

She winked. "You know the way."

Once she was gone, I put a call out to Timothy.

I told him the idea, asking Gloria to resign from the board in exchange for keeping the marriage fraud silent. We'd get the marriage annulled, and no one would be the wiser. Timothy seemed to ponder the idea.

"I've been thinking," he said. "Declaring the marriage would cause the addendum to go into effect."

"Gloria and Amber are the problems. If she's off the executive board, problem is solved."

"I was at the meeting, Damien. Grace Haas and Rachel Stokes voted against tabling the no-confidence vote."

"Those are only two votes with four in my favor. Five if we pick the right board member."

"There will need to be an election. Hell, the seat could remain open until the probation is complete. Talk to me about your parents. Ejecting the vice-chair shouldn't be done by proxy."

"Dad is still recovering and will be for a while. Mom is busy. And the idea isn't to eject Gloria but to convince her to resign."

"In my opinion," Timothy said, "we need to be prepared to take this a step further if she refuses the offer."

The door to my office opened and Johnathon rushed inside.

I covered the receiver of the phone and looked at my assistant. "What's happening?"

"Darius Sinclair is out front. He's live streaming on X, you know, Twitter."

"What the fuck?" I spoke into the phone. "Timothy, I'll call you back."

Johnathon turned up the volume and handed me his phone.

There was Darius, bruised face and all, standing in front of the fountain at Sinclair Corporate. Taking the phone in hand, I rushed across the room to the windows. There he was, standing on the pavers.

Red seeped into my vision as I turned my attention to the small screen in my hand.

"...address the rumors about what's happening at Sinclair Pharmaceuticals. It's true, my father, Derek Sinclair, the chairman of our board, suffered a health setback. While I'd willingly accept your thoughts and prayers, the reality is that my family—I use that term loosely—has chosen this time to further oust me from the company my father successfully ran for decades."

The stream was viral. And comments were adding up exponentially. From a quick scan, it seemed most were calling out Darius for being a whiny poor little rich man. However, there were also comments in support of his plight.

I turned to Johnathon. "Call security and get him off the property."

"Sir, do you think that's something you want live streamed?"

"Fuck, how long can he keep talking?"

"There's no limit on Twitter."

I was the CEO and a decision needed to be made. "Have him removed from the property. I'll call Dani." Currently, she was the chairwoman of the executive board.

Johnathon left as I called my sister on my cell phone. As soon as she answered, I asked, "Have you heard? Darius is airing family laundry on Twitter as we speak. He's live streaming from in front of this building."

"Fucking dick move," she mumbled. "What are you going to do?"

"I've sent security to remove him from the property."

"I have an idea. Meet me in ten minutes in the press room on one."

"What are you going to do?" I asked.

"Our brother is mentally unstable. It's time the world is aware."

Chapter 24

Gabriella

"What is happening?" I asked Johnathon as I slipped into the back of the Sinclair press room. The only warning I'd received was a text message from Damien telling me to hurry.

"Dr. Sinclair is about to address our shareholders and customers."

My brow furrowed. "Was this planned?"

Johnathon handed me his phone. The Twitter app was pulled up with a video paused.

My eyes widened. "Shit, is that Darius?"

Johnathon nodded. "You can watch it. The filming ends when Sinclair security and IMPD physically remove him from the property."

My heart sank. "Shit, this is bad. What did he say?"

We were speaking low as Damien and Dani were talking to members of the press and the cameras were being set up. If this was going to be like press releases from when I worked here, the broadcast would simultaneously run on multiple mediums and hopefully be picked up by larger news organizations.

"He rambled," Johnathon said. "Talked about Mr. Derek Sinclair."

I sucked my lower lip between my teeth. Marsha had been direct in not wanting personal information leaked. The public already knew more than she wanted them to know.

"His marriage?" I asked.

"I didn't hear that," he said. "I haven't listened to the entire rant."

Crossing my arms over my chest, I stood against the back wall. Finally, Damien looked up, his navy gaze meeting mine. The lines of worry and concern were again around his eyes. His jaw was clenched, and his neck strained.

Timothy Evans rushed into the room from the back door, not slowing until he was up front with Damien and Dani. He appeared to be quite animated in his discussion. I made my way closer.

"...bad idea. This will appear retaliatory," Timothy said.

"As CEO," Damien said, "and current chairwoman

of the board, it is within our rights to defend ourselves, our family, and our company. Sinclair Pharmaceuticals is more than a company; it's our legacy, and we won't allow Darius to burn it down around us."

Timothy was appealing to both of them. "Refrain from saying anything derogatory about Darius. He's baited you. He wants you to do something to give him the upper hand."

Dani nodded. As she turned, she saw me, and a feigned smile came to her face. "Welcome to the shit show." She lowered her volume. "Bet you're glad you're not married into this disastrous family."

"I'm not. I also know you, Damien, and your parents. The disastrous one is the one who is unraveling as we speak."

"He's probably calling a lawyer at this moment."

"Dr. Sinclair," a woman behind a camera called. "Please stand behind the podium and let us get the lighting right."

Dani squeezed my wrist. "Thanks for being here."

I nodded.

When I turned back to Johnathon, the lunch I'd eaten with Niles churned in my stomach. It wasn't Damien's assistant, but the woman next to him that caused my blood to boil. "What is she doing here?" I whispered to Damien.

"Fuck. I don't know how she knew about this."

I thought about Timothy's warning. "It was planned. Timothy was right. They knew this would be your next move."

Damien hurried from me to Dani. The two whispered back and forth.

"We're about to begin," the camerawoman yelled. "Quiet behind me. Places."

Damien took a step back, standing near Dani's shoulder.

"Three, two, one." The woman's hand went down.

"Let me thank you for watching," Dani began. "I'm Dr. Danielle Sinclair, one of the scientists here at Sinclair Pharmaceuticals and currently the chairwoman of our executive board. I'm here today with my brother, the CEO of Sinclair Pharmaceuticals, Damien Sinclair.

"The chairman's position on our board is held by our father, Derek Sinclair. I was asked to be his proxy for the time being. Today as CEO and chairperson, Damien and I would like to address some current issues and rumors. First and foremost, Sinclair Pharmaceuticals is stronger today than ever in our history. Second, and no less important, our father, Derek Sinclair, is recovering from an unexpected medical emergency. We ask for our father and mother that you please respect the privacy of our family during this difficult time."

"Dr. Sinclair," the few reporters present called out.

Dani lifted her hand. "Please let me finish. And then we'll open the floor to questions."

"The rumors of family strife are exaggerated and not entirely factual. Regardless of the validity of the statements you may have heard, Sinclair Pharmaceuticals is on an upward trajectory due in large part to the leadership of my brother, Damien Sinclair. Under his oversight, we have brought a landmark medication to the public. We are working on ways to make our medications less expensive and more readily available. Propanolol has caused a six-fold increase in profits over this time two years ago. Concerns over dividends do not reflect our income, but rather our commitment to research, development, and education. Damien and our father made the joint decision to lower shareholder dividends to allocate more available funding to the needs I just mentioned."

She turned and looked at Damien. "Would you like to address the public?"

A smile curled my lips as he stepped forward. All outward appearance of his stress was gone, hidden behind his professional mask. As his large hands gripped the sides of the podium, I was once again enthralled with his commitment to this company and his family.

"I am Damien Sinclair. I've been CEO of Sinclair Pharmaceuticals for the last four and a half years. Working side by side with my father and my sister has been my life's objective. Securing a revolutionary treatment for PTSD exceeded any goals I'd ever imagined. Propanolol has brought our little Indiana company to the forefront in pharmaceuticals. I believe we'll open the floor to questions."

"Mr. Sinclair," a gentleman said, standing. "Is it true you are still only a probationary CEO?"

"I assure you I am CEO. It is also true that our father set a probationary timeline, and I am almost to my goal."

"What does that mean for Darius Sinclair?"

"It has no bearing."

Another gentleman stood. "Darius Sinclair claims he has been ostracized by his family."

"Darius is our brother," Damien said.

Dani stepped forward. "We love and respect Darius and want him to get the help he needs."

My gaze turned to Timothy, who let his head fall forward.

"Is Darius ill? Mental health? Substance abuse?"

Dani lifted her hand. "Out of respect for the

privacy of our family, we will keep the questions to Sinclair Pharmaceuticals at this time."

The questions continued for another ten to fifteen minutes. Once in a while, someone would sneak in a question about Darius's live stream, but through it all, Dani and Damien refused to answer. Nothing was said about a wife or marriage.

"Thank you for coming," Damien said as the questions slowed. "We're done."

I waited as the reporters were led from the room. When I looked back to Johnathon, Amber was no longer beside him. I didn't know when she'd left. I'd been too busy watching and listening to the Sinclair duet.

Bringing my hands together, I mimicked clapping as Damien and Dani came my direction. "You were both amazing."

"Now we need to have an emergency executive board meeting and get everyone on the same page," Dani said.

"Here?" I asked.

"Virtual," she replied.

"What about Gloria's place on the board?" I asked, speaking to Damien.

"One fire at a time."

Timothy came close. "You made me nervous."

Dani smiled a sweet smile. "I want our brother to get whatever help he needs. Maybe an attorney."

"It was good," I said, thinking about her comment. "You insinuated but didn't specifically say what help he required."

"If anyone infers that is their issue. I didn't disparage or defame him."

We all looked at Timothy.

"I think you pushed the line, but an attorney would be hard-pressed to say you crossed it."

Chapter 25

Damien

Taking an extra-long look at her shapely legs as she climbed in, I helped Ella into my SUV. As I came around to the driver's side, and sat behind the steering wheel, Ella was buckling her seat belt. "You know, I didn't manipulate your flight to LA." I grinned. "Watching you fasten your seat belt reminded me of that fateful day."

"I wasn't supposed to be on that flight."

"I volunteered to go to LA with Van in hopes of seeing you, but that's where my input ended." I squeezed her hand. "This is meant to be, Ella. There's no denying it."

She leaned her head back against the seat as I drove out of the parking garage. It wasn't until we were under the sunny evening sky that she spoke. "How did the emergency board meeting go?"

"It was more symbolic. As chairwoman, Dani needed to inform the members of the day's happenings."

"Have you told your mom?"

I shook my head. "Mom told us to handle things. We are."

Ella turned, her smile growing. "You two are good together. I always admired your bond. Charlotte and I are close, but not like the two of you."

There wasn't a secret to our relationship. We'd always been there for one another as long as I can remember. There wasn't competition between us. If I gave that more thought, I might decide that Darius was our competition. Dad's second-marriage children against the son from his first marriage. That probably wasn't healthy, but who was I to judge?

"Did you get a chance to talk to Dani today?" I asked.

"Not about the night you broke things off with Amber. Last night, I wanted to ask her. Today, I decided I didn't need to."

I lifted my right hand. "I swear she would confirm my recollections."

"It doesn't matter. I choose to trust you."

"I don't deserve you, but that doesn't mean I'll ever let you go."

As we drove, Ella told me more about her

meeting with Millie Barns as well as her lunch with Niles. While I knew for certain there was nothing romantic between Ella and Niles, there was still a small part of me that wished her best friend was female. I wouldn't say that to her because the more I thought about it, the more I realized my best friend was female—my sister. And so was the person I wanted to spend my forever with.

"Did you get any work done with the campaign?"

"Talking with Millie helped me prioritize some things." She grinned. "I can't tell you more."

"What the hell?"

"Nope." She shook her head. "I decided that Millie either trusts me to pull this off or she gave me enough rope to hang myself. If it's the latter, I won't give her the satisfaction."

"She likes you."

Ella nodded. "She does. I also got the feeling that without Julia's call, things could have gone south fast. I want to make this work."

"I have no doubt." I turned her direction. "How about we spend tonight at our other place."

"Since we're only engaged, I think we can refer to our respective homes."

"Houses," I corrected. "A home is where we are together."

A smile curled her lips. "You're such a romantic."

"On Tuesdays, I have meals delivered. Currently, only three a week. We'll have to cook them, but all the ingredients are there."

"Cooking in that kitchen," she said, her words coming out singsong. "Yes."

"What about Duchess?"

"Let's stop by my place. I'll pack clothes for tomorrow and cosmetics. For today we can just set the automatic feeder. Hey, did the company do inspections of our security systems today?"

"They were supposed to." I shook my head. "I'm sorry, I have been crazy busy." I tilted my head toward the phone holder in the console. "Check my messages and see if they sent me a text."

Ella looked suspiciously at my phone. "You want me to look in your phone. That's a little personal, don't you think?"

"Last night, my tongue was in your cunt. I think we've passed the personal boundaries."

She scoffed. "When you put it like that." Ella picked up my phone. "What's your code?"

"1216." With a sly grin and a sideway glance, I watched for Ella's reaction.

"That's my birthday."

"Easy to remember."

"Oh," she said, "there is a message. It just says to call a man named Anthony."

"He's my contact. I'll call him in the morning."

"It's odd," Ella said. "My cameras have been off since I got out of the meeting with Millie."

"I'm sure it was them."

"You're probably right."

I pulled the SUV up to the curb near Ella's place. Although I'd shrugged it off, I didn't like hearing about her cameras. Looking up at the townhouse, everything appeared normal. "Maybe I should go in first."

"Why?"

"Your cameras," I reminded her.

"Don't do that, Damien. Stop adding worry where it doesn't exist. Don't you think we have enough shit going on?"

I lifted my hands. "Okay, guilty as charged. And besides, Darius was busy this afternoon in IMPD booking."

"You didn't have him charged," Ella said as she unlocked the front door.

"I did. We can drop the charges. I want him to know I'm serious."

"Duchess," Ella called as we entered the condo. "Will you go fill the automatic feeder while I go upstairs and pack?"

"Don't be long," I said, leaving a kiss on her lips. "Duchess," I called, thinking how the cat was usually our greeting committee. Maybe I was no longer novel. "Ella," I yelled as I entered the kitchen. "Ella, get down here."

Fuck.

I ran toward the steps as she was coming down.

"What's the matter?"

"The glass door to your deck is open."

Her eyebrows knitted together. "No, I wouldn't leave it open. Duchess. Oh my God. Duchess."

"Is anything else out of place?" I asked.

"Did that company do this? Damien, we need to find Duchess."

Did the security company leave a door open?

They better the fuck have not.

I pulled out my phone to call Anthony when Ella's desperate calls refocused me. Find the cat. Then call the security company.

I searched Ella's backyard. I suppose it could be called that. It was lush green grass and manicured bushes and flowerbeds all surrounded by a tall, stained fence. "Duchess."

Looking up at the height of the fence, I felt minutely better. Duchess couldn't jump over the privacy fence. I shone the light from my phone under the deck and called the cat's name. From the open door, I could hear Ella's voice grow more desperate.

Once inside, I closed the door and continued my search.

Under the sofa.

Behind the television stand.

Duchess was the only cat I knew. I had no idea where she would hide.

Finally, I began opening cabinets.

"Damien."

I turned to take in Ella's tear-streaked face. Simply seeing it made my heart break. Her hands were empty. "We'll find her," I said.

"She's not here."

Her hands trembled as I pulled her to me. "We'll find her." I stroked her hair. "Let me call the security company."

Ella nodded.

Taking out my phone, I hit Anthony's cell number. He answered on the second ring. "Did you do a security check of the three houses?"

"We were able to check Dr. Sinclair's place. She has a top-notch system in place. I have a few upgrades to recommend."

"What about Ms. Crystal's condo near downtown Carmel?"

"I thought she would have told you."

"Told me what?"

"When we arrived, she said to come back tomorrow."

My grip of the phone tightened as I pulled it from my ear and hit the speaker button. "Anthony, there's a problem. Ms. Crystal left her house this morning about seven thirty. What time did your men arrive?"

"Mr. Sinclair, I have the notes right here."

Ella's eyes were growing wider with each passing second. Her hand was near her mouth as if she wanted to cry out.

"What time?" I asked louder than before.

"Right here. The notes say Ms. Crystal was home and asked us to return tomorrow. The time is 9:20 a.m."

"Call the police," Ella said.

"Your people never came in the condo?" I asked for confirmation.

"No, sir."

"Can your men describe the woman they saw?"

"I'll call my guys and call you back."

"Hurry," I said, disconnecting the call.

My gaze met Ella's. "You should call the police. Someone was here."

"Who hurts a cat?"

"Duchess is fine. She probably got scared and ran out. We can call the humane society. I know, go on your neighborhood app and post a picture."

My phone buzzed.

It was a text message from Anthony.

"Still talking to them. Blond woman. Tall. I'll call soon."

Fuck.

Chapter 26

Gabriella

"What does it say?" I asked as a vein in Damien's forehead pulsated.

His gaze came my way, the shade darker than I'd ever seen. "It wasn't you."

"Was it...?" I couldn't bring myself to say her name.

She wouldn't.

"Amber," I finally said.

Damien nodded as he reached for my shoulders. "She's a bitch, but she wouldn't hurt Duchess. That's psychopath level." He looked around. "Why was she here?"

"Why?" My thoughts were racing. "What did Amber do? Did she take Duchess somewhere? Is Duchess abandoned on some country road or worse, by a busy street?"

"Wait, the humane society chipped her, right?" Damien asked.

"Yes, but it's a chip that needs to be read. It's not like she has an Apple watch that we can track."

"Apple collars. We're getting her one once she's home."

"Are those a thing?" My heart hurt. "What if we don't find her?"

"Ella, look around. Amber didn't want in your house for Duchess."

Slowly, I turned, taking in my living room and kitchen, down the hall to my office and foyer. "Nothing seems wrong."

"Let's go back upstairs."

I clung to Damien's arm as we climbed the stairs. "I don't know what I should be looking for."

Nothing was out of place, nothing that I hadn't disrupted while looking for Duchess. "Damien, I don't see anything." I frowned, my forehead furrowing and my eyebrows knitting together. "I hate that she was in here."

"Call the police," Damien said. "File a report. While you're doing that, I'll call local shelters and let them know Duchess is missing."

"I saw Amber during your press conference. I tried to ignore her." The memory came back. "She was smug. That's why I thought she expected you two to mess up. But she was smug because she knew what she'd done—that she'd been in my house."

As I pulled my phone from my purse, my hands trembled. "I don't know what to say." I searched for the non-emergency number and walked back toward my office. "Hello, I'd like to report a break-in..." I gave the dispatcher my address. When she asked if anything was missing, I choked on my answer. "My cat."

"Are you alone? Are you in the house?"

"I'm in the house." My gaze went to Damien. "I'm not alone."

"Are you certain no one is in your house?"

"Yes, we searched everywhere for our cat. The back door was left open."

"We're sending a unit right away."

My temples pounded as I disconnected the call.

Damien spoke, "The humane society is closed, but I left a message. Let's send out a post on your neighborhood app."

I handed Damien my phone. "You can do it."

Taking my phone, he wrapped his arm around me and pulled me to his side. "I love you."

Tears filled my eyes as I nodded against his suit coat. "What if she's scared?"

"Duchess isn't scared. Wherever she is, she's in

complete control of the situation. She's probably bored."

"After I left you," I said, "she kept me sane. I know she's a cat and it sounds stupid, but I talked to her."

"You told her bad things about me?" Damien asked.

I sighed with a nod. "She was a safe listener."

"I don't know what Amber's plan was, but I can't believe it was to cause harm to Duchess."

We both turned at the ringing of my doorbell.

"That was fast," Damien said.

"The cameras," I said, remembering they were out. "She disconnected my cameras."

"Is there footage on your doorbell of her coming up the front stoop?"

The doorbell rang again.

Damien walked toward the door. After checking the sidelight, he opened the door. The policeman was in full uniform.

"We had a report of a break-in," he said.

"Yes," Damien replied. "Please come in."

"I'm looking for a Gabriella Crystal."

"That's me," I said from down the hallway. "It was my back door that was open."

"Do you recall leaving it open?"

"No, sir. It was open when we got home."

"Any signs of forced entry?"

There wasn't.

Damien and I answered Officer Johnson's questions. He even walked around the entire house with us, checking closets and looking under beds.

"You said your security cameras were turned off?" the policeman asked.

"Yes, they stopped working sometime this morning."

"Did you lose feed from your nanny cam?" he questioned as he pointed to a nightlight. "My wife bought some just like these. You can't even tell they're damn cameras. They're great with teenagers."

"Nanny cam?" I looked at Damien and shook my head. "Did the security company install these? I didn't, and I didn't notice them earlier."

"There were a few downstairs, too," the officer said.

"Bitch," Damien mumbled under his breath. "The company didn't install them. They never were able to access the inside of your house."

Together we went room to room. Officer Johnson collected all the cameras—seven in total.

I checked the recorded video from my doorbell. There wasn't footage of Amber coming to the house before the cameras stopped working, but there was a nice one of her earlier this morning.

Officer Johnson looked at my phone. "And you believe this is who broke in and planted the cameras?"

"I do," I answered. "And took my cat." I hoped she took her and that Duchess wasn't alone and scared.

"There was a security company that came by to check her security system," Damien offered, "and they told me that Ella answered the door. She didn't. She wasn't home. The description matches this woman." He pointed toward my phone. "Her name is Amber Wilmott."

By the time Officer Johnson left, my head was throbbing, and my stomach was unsettled. "She wanted to spy on us. That's sick."

"There must be something she wants to learn." He sighed. "Do you want to walk around the neighborhood?"

"I do."

The spring temperatures were in a consistent warming pattern. As we walked up and down the neighborhood sidewalks, we met people walking their dogs and parents with children in yards. Each person we saw, we stopped and asked if they'd seen a black cat with a sparkling pink collar.

The answer was always the same.

No one had seen her.

When we returned to my place, I was overwhelmed with the emptiness that went along with Duchess's absence. "I don't want to go to your place. I want to be here in case she comes home."

Damien nodded.

"Will you stay here?"

"Of course," he said. "I need to pick up the dry cleaning that was dropped off at my place today. I'll get us dinner on my way back. Keep the doors locked and only open them to a beautiful green-eyed black kitty."

More tears came as I tried to breathe. "What if she's gone?"

"I refuse to believe that."

"I wish I were as stubborn as you."

Damien cupped my cheek. "I refused to believe you were gone, and now you're back. Duchess will come back too."

"I don't know. She listened to all those bad things about you."

"And she welcomed me back with purrs and head rubs."

After Damien left, I double-checked both doors. For a few minutes, I stood in my living room and cried. I'd like to say I was productive in some manner, but I wasn't.

What kind of a monster harms a cat?

What did Amber hope to learn from spying?

They were the questions on repeat in my head. Beyond the glass door, night was beginning to fall in my backyard. Opening the sliding door, I sat on the step to the deck, looking out over the grass as lightning bugs began to blink in the dimming light.

"Duchess, come home."

I remembered the neighborhood app and decided to check to see if we'd gotten any responses. My eyes blurred as I read the messages. No one had seen her, but they all wished me luck and offered their sympathies.

"She's not gone," I mumbled, hoping I was speaking life to the dream.

It was as I was pouring a glass of wine with the back door still open that my phone rang. It was a video call. It was Damien.

"Hi," I said.

His image was pixelated, but I couldn't believe my eyes.

"Duchess," I screamed. "Where did you find her?"

"Asleep on my bed."

"What the hell?" I smiled as she stretched her neck and rubbed her head across Damien's cheek. "She's not hurt?"

"She seems no worse for wear from her journey. Remember the security company?"

I nodded.

"They couldn't get in my place. The deadbolt was locked."

"Amber was at your place?"

"I have video proof and a gallon bag full of nanny cams to prove it. Do you want me to come back with Duchess, or do you want to come here?"

Amber had been in both houses. "We aren't safe either place."

"We are. The security company is on their way. My locks here are getting changed tonight."

My headache was waning. "I'll be there. I can drive myself," I added before he mentioned a bodyguard.

"Text when you leave and if it takes longer than eleven minutes, I'm coming for you."

Damien was waiting outside as I pulled into his driveway. His smile was almost the best thing I'd seen all day. Second to the silky black cat in his kitchen.

"I brought some of Duchess's essentials," I said as I scooped her into my arms. "Did that mean woman take you on a car ride? I hope you vomited all over her car." I looked up at Damien. "She's not a fan of car rides."

He scratched between her ears. "I'll get the things out of your car."

It was almost nine at night by the time the security company had changed all of Damien's locks and his garage-door codes. Duchess was loving the increased square footage, and I'd begun cooking one of the meals Damien had delivered when he came up behind me and wrapped his arms around me.

"This feels right."

I laid my head back against his solid chest. "It does." Setting down the spoon, I spun and looked up at him. "You make me feel safe."

"You shouldn't," he said with a sly grin.

"I shouldn't?"

"No, you're not safe with me. I want to do bad things to you later tonight."

I tipped my head to his chest. "I trust you."

Chapter 27

Damien

The idea of cohabitation had never been as important to me as it was tonight. Although I had plenty of ideas of what I wanted to do to and with Ella, the weight of the day and the range of emotions had taken their toll. After dinner, I took a quick shower. Standing under the spray, I concentrated on the one thing I could control.

Our safety.

Ella was here.

Duchess was here.

I was exactly where I wanted to be.

I would stop at nothing to maintain that sense of security.

With droplets of water dripping from my hair and a towel around my waist, I walked into the bedroom. That well-being I desired was personified in the room before me. Golden illumination shone from the lamps on the bedside stands on both sides of the bed. Duchess was sleeping, curled into a circle near Ella's feet.

Ella sat against a stack of pillows, her computer in her lap. Her face was pink and freshly washed of cosmetics. Her long dark hair was down, cascading over her shoulders. It was her nightgown that made me smile. She was wearing one of my many Indianapolis Colts t-shirts, and it had never looked better.

"Nice nightgown."

Her smile lit up the room. "I packed so fast that I forgot a nightgown."

"Did you forget panties too? Because I'm a big fan of easy access."

She closed her laptop screen as she scanned me from my wet hair to my toes. "Speaking of easy access, I'm waiting for you to drop the towel."

Of course I did.

The plush towel fell near my feet.

I lowered my tone. "I hope you like what you see."

Ella's smile grew. "Very much and I like that you're showing it to me."

"Only you." Ella knew me better than anyone. Nudity was perfect when a woman was stark naked.

I'd be okay with making that a house dress code. When it came to me, it was another story. I liked the power of inequality.

From my perspective, allowing a woman to see me as I was now was more than sexual. It evened the playing field, and I wasn't about even, not with anyone other than Ella.

I was about to throw back the covers and climb into bed exactly as I was when my phone rang. Ella leaned across the bed to read the screen. "It's Marsha."

"Saved by the bell," I said as I nodded toward the phone. "Answer it for me. I'll put on my boxers."

Ella laughed. "Talking to your mom naked is..." Her nose scrunched. "Wait, if I answer your phone, she'll know we're together."

"Yeah, she still thinks we're married."

"Oh, that's right." Ella pursed her lips.

"Hi, Marsha." I heard her say as I went into the large closet and slipped into a clean pair of boxers. As I came back out, she said, "That's good news. Here, let me pass you to Damien."

I took the phone. "Hi, Mom. What's the good news?"

Mom proceeded to tell me what she'd no doubt just explained to Ella. Dad was progressing. His blood pressure and pulse oximeter readings were good. It meant his heart was doing its job. On top of that, they'd lowered his pain medicine. After the update, she added, "I read about the news conference."

"It's nothing, Mom. Dani and I have everything under control."

"I figured you did."

I almost mentioned Ella's and my invalid marriage and the one with Amber. However, as I constructed the sentences in my head, I decided Mom had enough concerns. I'd rather tell her after the annulment was filed.

After disconnecting the call, I made my way beneath the covers. Ella laid her laptop on the bedside stand and turned off the lamp. As darkness covered the room, she curled against my side, her head on my shoulder.

"I don't think I would want to be alone after what Amber did."

Wrapping my arm around her, I pulled her close. "You're not alone. You never will be if I have my way."

"Don't you always get your way?"

"Not always, but my average isn't bad. Sometimes it takes longer than I want." Like having you back in my arms.

I kissed the top of her head.

"Why spy on us?" she asked.

"I've been thinking about it and I've come up with a few options. (A) she's obsessed with me."

"Yeah, because all women are."

"(B) She—and maybe my brother—want proof of Dwain Welsh's concern."

Ella lifted her head. "That I'm sharing trade secrets with you from the coalition?"

I nodded.

"And taking Duchess?" she asked.

"A power play."

She laid her head back on my shoulder. "I'm exhausted. Will you hold me as I fall asleep?"

"There's no place I'd rather be."

Ella rolled to her side, and I rolled with her. With her back to my front and my arms around her, I knew of something I wanted but couldn't have. I wanted to take away the horrible hours we spent thinking that Duchess was missing, the way Ella's tears streamed down her cheeks, and the sadness in her voice. The longer I held Ella, the more determined I became to bring a stop to this disastrous situation with Darius and Amber.

The next morning, I'd awakened to the email Amber said would arrive.

Ella's and my marriage was invalid.

I was already married.

As I walked with Ella out to the driveway, she

reached for my hand. We'd both had visual confirmation of Duchess, who happened to be lying in a beam of morning sunlight in the library.

"Damien, be careful," Ella said before sliding into the back seat of Deidra's car.

I held the door open and peered inside. Wearing one of the outfits I'd chosen for our trip to Ashland, Ella was dressed for her day at the office. With her hair styled up, she was breathtakingly beautiful. Then again, this morning with sleep in her eyes and her warm, soft body at my side, she was also striking.

"I will. I'll see you at Corporate." I hadn't told Ella my plans for the morning, but that didn't stop her from figuring them out.

"Please don't get in a fight with your brother."

I clenched my jaw. "It's not my goal."

Ella waved as they pulled away. For a moment, I stood there, contemplating my next move.

I hadn't been to Amber's place since the night I left her.

That night, I'd given her back her key. It hadn't occurred to me until last night that she'd never returned mine. That was how she had gotten into my house. It wasn't technically breaking and entering if she had a key. That didn't explain how she got into Ella's place. As I was driving to Amber's place, I wondered if she'd be home or if Darius would be there. The closer I got, the more I hoped I'd see both.

My phone rang through the speakers of my SUV. The name on the screen was *Anthony*. I hit the green icon on the steering wheel. "What do you have for me?"

"The woman entered Ms. Crystal's house by blocking the lock of the front door."

"How did she block it?"

"It's simple. When Ms. Wilmott was at the door earlier in the morning, while Ms. Crystal went back inside, Ms. Wilmott placed a thin magnetic strip over the strike plate, thus blocking the latch bolt from engaging. Ms. Crystal probably thought she'd locked the door, but in reality, the latch never engaged."

"How the fuck would Amber know how to do that?" I asked.

"She probably watched a YouTube video. It's an effective means to prevent someone from securing a lock."

I shook my head. "Do you have proof?"

"I know I'm correct. There's limited physical evidence. She undoubtedly took the strip with her after she left. There is residue and in the original video of their morning altercation, I've been able to slow it down. There are a few frames where she appears to be touching the doorjamb. Would my evidence hold up in a court of law? Doubtful."

Fuck that.

I was the judge and the jury in this case. Amber was lucky I wasn't also an executioner.

"Is Ms. Crystal's house now secure?"

"Yes, sir."

"Are her cameras up and running?"

"With the upgrades we discussed. My crew and I are on our way to your house now to complete the additions we discussed last night."

I said the first thing that came to mind, "Don't let the cat out."

"I didn't see that you had a cat."

"Well, I do now. She used up one of her nine lives yesterday. I'd rather her stay at eight."

"I'll let my crew know."

"Contact me once the job is finished," I said.

As our call disconnected, I entered the same neighborhood I left over a year ago. Though Amber worked between Chicago and Indianapolis, the last I recalled, her residence was in Indy. I approached the home where she'd lived. The door to Amber's garage was closed, hiding whether her car or Darius's was inside. The clock on the dashboard told me it wasn't yet eight in the morning.

"Be home," I said to myself as I got out of the vehicle.

The walk up the sidewalk was a sick sort of déjà vu. As I scanned the front of her place, I deduced that not much had changed in the past year. With pent-up energy, I rang the doorbell and waited. I rang it again. Peering through the sidelight, I saw movement. This time, I banged on the door.

"Open the door, Amber. You fucking wanted to see me. I'm here."

The door opened from within.

From her appearance, she was on her way out for the day.

"Lower your voice. I have neighbors."

"We'll explain that it's a domestic issue. I'm here to talk to my wife."

Chapter 28

Damien

Amber's green gaze narrowed. I'd seen this woman happy. What I was viewing now wasn't even close to happy.

"Let me in," I demanded.

"I have a job to get to."

I reached high for the doorjamb. "I don't give a fuck. We're going to talk."

"Fine," she said, taking a step back.

Following her inside, it took all my willpower not to physically attack her for what she'd done. When it came to women, I wasn't a violent man. I liked control in the bedroom, but any pain to pleasure was consensual. No part of me wanted to bring Amber pleasure.

My hands balled to fists at my sides as I maintained a calm appearance.

By Amber's alarmed expression, there was the possibility that I wasn't appearing as calm as I thought.

"Damien?" She lifted her hand. "Don't touch me."

My jaw clenched as I continued to walk forward and she backward. It was a tango with the sexual overture replaced by rage. Both were highly volatile emotions, either one capable of scorching flames that could leave destruction in its wake.

"You don't want me to touch you," I said louder than I planned. "You faked our marriage license. You broke into Ella's house and into my house and planted cameras. You stole her cat."

Amber's eyes opened wide as her back collided with a wall.

I continued, "You obviously wanted my attention. You have it now, Amber. Are you happy?"

She held her chin high in defiance. "I didn't steal a cat. I relocated it."

"You broke the law. Relocating the cat was your cowardly way of giving us a threat or a distraction."

She shook her head. "You can't prove any of what you said."

"The police have the cameras. They can establish purchase history and fingerprints. When we press charges, you'll be sitting in jail."

Amber lifted her chin higher.

My gaze went to her neck as I imagined my fingers wrapping around her throat, squeezing as her face reddened...

Instead, I took a step back. "You and I are having our marriage annulled."

"Providing the board with our marriage is your only chance to avoid the no-confidence vote. Don't you see, it will save you."

My nose wrinkled. "Why marry Darius?"

"To get your attention."

"You're fucking sick, Amber. I'm not worried about the no-confidence vote. You see, Timothy Evans is currently meeting with your mother."

Amber laid her hand on my arm.

I pulled my arm away. "The no touching goes both ways."

"My mom," she said, "is innocent. She thinks we married and then had a fight."

"You're lying. Your mother was involved in the fucking fraud. Does the name Vallencia sound familiar?"

She shrugged. "I don't know. I work with a lot of people."

"It seems as if you'd recall the officiant at our wedding. That's right, our wedding never happened. Your mother paid Vallencia off with cash and helped get him an extension on his visa."

Amber shook her head. "None of that is true."

My voice boomed, echoing through the living room. "It's all fucking true." I stopped and took a breath. "Your mother has served Sinclair Pharmaceuticals faithfully for many years. She is facing a choice. Either she resigns voluntarily as an honored member of our executive board, or I'll take everything public. I'll drag you and Gloria through the courts. Our marriage will not only be annulled based on the proof that our marriage was a fraud, but the once-respected name of Wilmott will be muddied. I'm sure the good senator would roll over in his fucking grave having the public learn you broke into homes and planted bugs so you could get off on Ella's and my sex life."

"That's not why. Darius thought..." She shook her head. "Believe whatever you want."

"Darius was the one who put you up to breaking into our homes?"

"Damien, think about this. Even if Mom's off the board, the no-confidence vote will have to progress. I didn't want you to find out about the marriage like this. I thought we could make it work. I wanted to help you."

"You wanted to help yourself. Gloria wanted to tell the world her daughter married a Sinclair. No, not *a* Sinclair. Me. Damien. We all know Darius isn't the same catch." I looked around. "Where is my brother?"

"Not here."

A sinister smile curled my lips. "Did he leave you when he learned you'd played him? Or doesn't he have the balls to leave. You left him, pledging to make our marriage work. No, you were doing his dirty work. What does he have on you?"

She looked down at her hands and back up. "I do want our marriage to work. And it can't if you're working with her. I agreed that finding incriminating evidence to take to the coalition would get her out of our lives."

Amber's focus brought my attention to the ring she was still wearing, the one Darius gave her. "She is Gabriella, and she is very much in my life." I motioned between the two of us. "Our marriage isn't happening. And if you wanted that, why are you still wearing his ring?"

She lifted her hand. "It's beautiful. And I didn't *play* Darius. I *like* him."

"You like him." I pressed my lips together and nodded. "Then let's get our annulment and you two can live happily ever after."

"He's not..." She looked pleadingly toward me. "He needs to feel like he's part of the family."

"Screwing my legal wife isn't close enough for him?"

Amber huffed. "Don't you care about him? He's your brother."

"I do. I care that he leaves Dad and Mom alone. I care that he goes on with his own fucking life and agrees that his involvement in Sinclair Pharmaceuticals is over. If he wanted one big happy family, he wouldn't have spent the last thirty-eight years trying to one-up me or catch me at something and fail at every fucking juncture."

"That's just what brothers do."

I shook my head. "It's not. Darius has felt incompetent ever since I was born. He knew he could never be me. I had both parents loving one another. You know why I walked out of here that night a year ago?"

"Your note said things moved too fast."

"My parents," I said. "I knew that I'd never have what they have, with you."

Amber looked down. "You don't have to be cruel."

"I'm being honest. And as for siblings, Dani and I know what that means. We have one another's back. We support our parents the best we can. It's always been a competition with Darius." I scanned Amber up and down. "I'm sure he thought he hit fucking pay dirt when he landed you. Did you tell him you left me?"

"When Darius tried to run Sinclair, he had too much pressure. He's ready now."

I couldn't believe my ears. "Why the fuck are you fighting for him?"

"I like him. I'm worried about him. If he could co-CEO with you, he would feel redeemed."

"It's not my fucking problem if he feels redeemed."

The phone in my suit coat pocket buzzed. I pulled it from inside the coat and brought the screen to life. I had two unread messages. Both made me smile. The first was from Ella.

"Oh, control freak, my love. I'm in my office at Corporate. Tell me you're okay. I don't want to have to bail you out of jail."

The second was from Timothy.

"It is with great sadness that Mrs. Gloria Wilmott announces her resignation from the Sinclair Pharmaceutical executive board. She reflects fondly on her time with this company and is satisfied that through her tenure, Sinclair Pharmaceuticals has become a thriving competitor."

. . .

I reacted to Ella's message with a heart emoji and to Timothy's with a thumbs up.

"Damien?" Amber asked.

"It's over. Your mother has stepped down. Dani will call a meeting of the board and the no-confidence vote will be stricken from the minutes. If Darius brings it up again, I'll press charges against both of you for breaking, entering, and planting recording devices without our consent. Timothy has begun the filing for the annulment. You won't fight it."

"If we stay married, you could get out of the probationary period."

I shook my head. "I'm not worried. I have five more months. Even if Ella and I wed before that, I'm not bringing up the addendum. I'm fucking good at what I do. I'll have the permanent title."

She tilted her head. "I really wanted us to work. I thought you'd come back."

"Ella is my someone. I've known that since the first time I saw her. I was wrong to encourage a relationship between the two of us, you and me. For that, Amber, I'm sorry. I should have been going after her."

"I never thought you'd show up with her. I

couldn't believe it when you came to the hospital. I thought you two were over."

I never gave up.

It was one fateful flight that brought us back together.

"Not over," I said. "Just rekindling what we had and making it stronger."

Chapter 29

Gabriella
One month later

"**W**hy is Mr. Welsh pulling out of the coalition?" I asked Julia through the phone.

"It isn't because of the campaign. I believe he is still working with Beta Kappa Phi."

"He is," I said, "with another manager." Thank goodness. "Did he give you a reason?"

"He told me something in confidence."

"Then I won't ask. I know what it's like being put on the spot."

Julia laughed. "Is that a Damien reference?"

"Oh, you know it."

"I do know the pressure. Van can be very persuasive. Honestly, you'll learn about Welsh's reasoning soon enough."

My curiosity was piqued. "I might say I won't tell Damien, but I probably will."

"That's why I want to tell you. Dwain and Darius Sinclair are partnering with a new LLC, an offshoot of Moon Medical."

"Really?"

"They're working on the contracts, but it seems that through the coalition, Dwain realized how lucrative Body Kindness is. It's a different market. There is less stringent testing and no patent BS. Make a statement about not claiming results somewhere in a lengthy insert and you're covered for liability. The healthy mind and body craze is going strong. There isn't the work like you're doing to get prescriptions, just infomercials to get the word out. Their new products will be in competition with Perry, and therefore, he must leave our coalition."

"Have you told the Cades?" I asked. The CEOs of Perry and Body Kindness.

"You have access to their revenue. They'll be fine. They have a recognizable and reputable name with Body Kindness. I can't imagine they'll even notice the competition."

"Thank you for letting me know. I'll make the necessary changes in the campaign and send you a breakdown."

"Even though this campaign was our husbands' idea—oh, sorry, your *fiancé's*."

I chuckled, looking down at my diamond ring.

Julia went on, "...I couldn't be happier with the headway you've made in a short time."

The door to my office opened and a handsome man with a dark-blue stare entered. There was a gleam in his eyes that told me he was up to something. "Speaking of that fiancé, he just entered my office. I better go."

"It was nice to talk to you," Julia said before disconnecting the call.

I hung up my desk phone and scanned the man who'd awakened me this morning with his face between my legs. It was admittedly a great way to wake. Damien was dapper in his suit pants, button-up shirt, and tie. "Why do you look like the cat who just ate the canary?" I asked.

"No canary. I had some great pussy this morning."

Shaking my head, I stood and walked around my desk. "Inappropriate, Mr. Sinclair."

"Who were you talking to?"

"Julia Sherman. There are about to be some changes with the coalition."

He stood straighter. "Then I should know."

"Confidential."

Damien's smile simmered as he scanned me up and down.

Without a word, my nipples grew painfully hard. "What are you thinking?" I asked.

"What I can do to make you talk."

"I'm sure you'll get it out of me soon enough. Now, the canary look?"

He showed me the paper in his hand. "Guess what this is?"

"Your dad's get-out-of-rehab paper?"

"No, but that should be coming soon." He handed me the letter.

I opened it and scanned the heading. "It's from Superior Court No. 1 Hamilton County." My eyes widened as I looked up at Damien. "It's the annulment."

"It is. I'm a free man."

"Not for long," I said before pushing up on my toes and giving him a kiss.

Damien snaked his arm around my waist. "This time when we say our vows, I'm not letting you get out of it."

The warmth in my cheeks was probably letting Damien know I was thinking about another time I couldn't get out. Slowly, we'd been playing with some of the restraints Damien had mentioned over a month ago. These were the ones in his closet. And yes, I couldn't get out of them, but I wasn't complaining.

"What are you thinking?" he asked.

I shook my head. "I was thinking that it's been kind of hot knowing I was sleeping with a married man." I shrugged. "I'm not sure sex will be as great now that you're free."

Damien pulled me closer, flattening my breasts against his chest as his other hand slid behind my neck. Our lips collided seconds before his tongue teased mine. I willingly granted him entrance. He tasted of toothpaste and my body warmed, melding against his. Soft against hard, our attraction was combustible. The more time we spent together, the less ability either one had to keep our hands off one another.

A small spark could ignite a raging wildfire.

When Damien pulled away, he lifted his eyebrows. "Not as hot?"

My cheeks rose in a smile. "I was wrong. If you were any hotter, I may end up being burned."

"Fire play. I've never done that."

"No," I said definitely. "And we won't."

"I think this news is worthy of a celebration."

I turned toward my desk. "Well, it's after five o'clock, and I was just thinking about going home and—"

Damien's lips met mine.

"I love when you call our house home."

"It's Duchess's fault. She's gotten used to more space and well...she's spoiled."

"Spoiling pussies is my favorite thing to do. Tonight, I'm taking my fiancée out on the town and tomorrow, we can wed."

"Oh no. After explaining the whole mess to our mothers, they made me promise a real wedding."

Damien cupped my cheek. "You deserve the best wedding ever."

Over an hour later, back at home, Damien was in his downstairs office, and I was upstairs, getting ready for our celebratory dinner. In the month since Duchess made her unexpected move to the big house, many of my clothes and personal items had followed.

Eventually, we'll put the condo up for sale. I was holding onto it out of fear for what Amber may do. Remarkably, she'd kept her word and not fought the annulment. I think her reasoning was similar to her mother's. They knew that if the whole story got out, they would be the ones who were cast in an unflattering light.

Now that the annulment had been granted, we were a step closer.

Wearing a towel, following my quick shower, I

stood in the large closet—basically the size of my bedroom in the condo—deciding what to wear. I ran my fingers over the dresses that seemed to multiply while we were at work. I'd complained at first, but Damien convinced me that he did enjoy dressing me. A deep-blue dress caught my eye.

The tags were still attached.

Refusing to look at the price, I lifted the dress in front of me in the full-length mirror, thinking how spectacular his shopper was, even better than I was at getting my size right. Truthfully, I wasn't a big shopper. If buying me clothes made Damien happy, and at the same time kept me out of the shops, it was a win-win situation.

Damien met me in the bathroom as I was applying lipstick.

"I just spoke to Julia. I think I know your confidential news."

I met his stare in the mirror. "Moon Medical."

Damien nodded as he stood behind me and wrapped his arms around my waist, peering at us in the reflection. "You're gorgeous, Ella. That dress makes your eyes shine."

Spinning in his grasp, I undid his tie. "I saw a blue tie in the closet that will match."

Damien's grin grew. "Are you dressing me now?"

"Currently, I'm undressing you." I pulled the tie from his collar. "But yes, I like dressing you, too."

As we were about to go into the garage, I paused and opened my small purse. "I have something for you."

"A gift?"

"Yes, celebrating your annulment." I handed him the lace panties I'd taken off after work, not replacing them for our night out.

Damien lifted them to his nose. "Good girl. These have been worn."

I shook my head. "I thought that in case you were going to make inappropriate demands, I'd let you know, I'm okay with them."

He reached for my elbow. "Let's get dinner and come back here. I have some very inappropriate suggestions."

"Celebrate first."

"Oh, you'll be celebrating, I promise."

So cocky and confident.

Chapter 30

Damien

"I've never eaten here," Ella said as we walked up to the 1920's Mediterranean-style villa in the Meridian-Kessler area of Indianapolis.

"It's one of my favorite restaurants."

"Mr. Sinclair," Evelyn, the hostess, greeted as we entered. "When I saw your name on our reservation list, I saved your favorite table for you."

"Thank you, Evelyn," I said with a bow. "This is Ella, my soon-to-be bride."

Evelyn extended her hand and Ella shook it. "Welcome, Ms. Ella. You have quite a man."

As Ella looked up at me, I was the one to respond. "I have an amazing woman."

"Come this way," Evelyn said.

"She likes you," Ella whispered.

Placing my hand in the small of Ella's back, I softly laughed. Evelyn was older than my parents. With her rhinestone glasses and fancy dresses, she enjoyed hitting on all the wealthy men dining at Mama Carolla's.

And Dani thought men were sexist.

Evelyn led us through the hallway of what had once been a home and out onto a paved patio. Lights were strung overhead and romantic music filtered through the air. The table Evelyn saved was a table for four nestled between a vine-covered hedge and a large fountain.

I pulled out the chair near the hedge for Ella and took the one to her side.

Once Evelyn was gone, I turned and whispered. "I have thought of nothing but your gift since we left home."

Ella's smile grew as she sat taller. "You don't make me disappear, Damien. You help me shine, and I see that now. You make me see the world differently, and I'm seeing you differently."

"Look over there," I motioned with my chin. The lights in the fountain changed with the music coming through the speakers.

"It's beautiful."

"This is my favorite table because I can see others, but with the vines and fountain, we're less visible." Laying my hand on her knee, I gathered the material of her dress.

Ella's eyes opened wide. "What are you doing?"

"Something inappropriate. Since this is one of my favorite places to eat, I want to taste my favorite juice."

Pink filled Ella's cheeks as the waiter arrived.

After ordering our wine and appetizers, I handed Ella a napkin.

"What is that for?"

"Stifle your scream. We don't want to draw attention."

"Damien, you are not going to finger me in a restaurant."

"I am."

As she turned one way and the next, I knew she was contemplating what I'd said. She was deciding if we could do it—if it could be our secret. The way her breathing deepened and the hue of her décolletage grew a brighter pink, I had my answer.

"Admit it. You want to come, right here."

"Damien, what if people know?"

"No one will know. Our inappropriate secret." I leaned closer and whispered. "You started this with your gift. I know you're not wearing panties. How did you expect me to go all evening without touching you?"

"Anticipation," she said.

I slid my hand beneath the hem of her dress.

Ella's eyes widened as she took the napkin in hand.

"Spread those sexy legs."

The muscles beneath my touch relaxed as she slowly adjusted. I was almost to my goal when our wine arrived. When my gaze met Ella's, she had the most stunning smile as a nervous giggle bubbled from her lips.

"Sir, would you like to taste the cabernet?"

One of my hands was occupied. "The lady may taste."

"Oh," Ella said flustered. "Okay." She took a deep breath and laid her hands on the table.

As the waiter handed Ella a wine goblet, I moved my fingers higher.

Ella clamped her thighs together as she took the goblet, swirled the wine, and made a show of enjoying the bouquet.

"I can smell the aroma," I said. "I'm sure it tastes as good as it smells."

Ella's expression told me that she knew I wasn't

talking about the wine. After a deep breath, she took a sip. "It's very good."

Her legs relaxed and I went higher.

It was as I brushed over her clit that Ella reached for the napkin.

"Is everything to your liking?" the waiter asked.

I turned to Ella. "Is it?"

She nodded and hummed.

I spoke to the waiter. "We're officially engaged. She's just excited."

"Oh," he said, "it is a celebration. We will bring you a special dessert after dinner."

"Thank you." After he left us, I leaned closer and whispered, "I'm about to have my dessert first."

As Ella's breathing deepened, she sat forward giving me better access.

One swipe and another.

Warmth covered my finger. "Inappropriate," I said.

Her eyes came to me.

"Coming on my fingers. You're soaked."

She closed her eyes as I continued the ministrations. It was as I pressed and rolled her clit that Ella brought the napkin to her mouth, not before I saw she was biting her lip. Watching her come was one of my favorite pastimes and watching her try to stifle her responsive and sensual reaction was even better.

"Oh shit," she mumbled as her body trembled. She pressed her hand against the table.

"You are stunning." I removed my hand and licked my fingers. "Yes, all of my favorites in one place. We can cancel the dessert—I had mine first."

"Oh my God," she whispered. "I can't believe we just..." She looked in all directions.

"No one was watching. They should have. You're better than anything on the menu."

Ella shook her head and lifted her glass of wine. "If there's a wet spot on my dress, you're giving me your jacket to leave."

"Your dress is lined for a reason."

She bowed her head as a new level of pink filled her cheeks. "Now I'm going to think of that every time I wear a lined dress."

"Good." I lifted my wine glass. "To many more inappropriate adventures."

Ella lifted her glass and we both took a sip.

"You are a lot to handle, Damien."

"And you're the only one who can do it."

Night had fallen by the time we drove home. As we traveled north from stoplight to stoplight, I said, "You are spectacular. When do you want to get married?"

"There's something else I want to do now."

"You don't want to marry?"

"I do," she said, unbuckling her seat belt.

"What are you doing?"

"Payback."

Fuck.

Chapter 31

Gabriella

"*E*lla," Damien said, as I unbuckled his belt, "I'm driving."

"Mr. Sinclair, I want your cock. Tell me you don't want to come."

He flashed me a devious grin. "Using my own words against me."

It was my turn to be in control. "Move your seat back."

"Fuck, Ella."

Maybe it was the wine or the atmosphere of the restaurant. It was more likely my first public orgasm; whatever the muse, I wanted to give Damien a taste of what I experienced.

"I'm not turning you down." He hit a button, moving the driver's seat back.

I took one more look out the windshield, seeing

the streetlights along Keystone Avenue. It wasn't as if we were on an interstate. There were businesses and houses all around. Other cars passed, and we had a series of stoplights in our future.

A smile came to my lips at the growing bulge beneath his pants.

Yes, Damien sought control, but what was happening to his body was my doing. Getting to my knees on the seat, I quickly unfastened his button and lowered the zipper. Pushing the silky material of his boxer briefs down, I freed his growing cock and lapped the shining tip.

"Fuck," he growled, tightening his grip of the steering wheel.

Despite the cool breeze of the air conditioning, my body warmed as I savored his spicy taste. "Eyes on the road, Mr. Sinclair."

I wrapped my lips around him, slowly sliding down his length and not stopping until the head of his penis hit the back of my throat.

Curses filled the car.

Up and down, I bobbed my head. Using my tongue, I teased the tip before tightening my lips and sucking. In mere seconds, his penis grew both in length and girth, hard as steel. I continued licking and moving my head.

Damien's hand came to the back of my head as his hips began to buck. "Fuck, Ella. Take it. All of it."

Faster I sucked and bobbed, the pressure from his hand keeping me focused as my nipples tightened and more moisture dampened my thighs. Damien's ragged breathing and movements of his hips let me know that he was close. Unbelievably, so was I. This was hotter than I imagined. And I'd been imagining it ever since I came at the restaurant.

I felt the car swerve before Damien slammed on the brakes.

"Fucking Christ," he called out as both hands came to my head, his fingers entangling in my hair.

I couldn't stop if I wanted.

I didn't want to stop.

The knowledge that I was making the great Damien Sinclair lose control was like jet fuel coursing through my bloodstream. I was on autopilot as I continued my mission. Reaching for his balls, I twisted and rubbed.

His hips jumped as he cursed the seat belt.

A deep, resonating roar echoed throughout the automobile as he came, filling my mouth with his salty seed. Lap after lap, I swallowed as the tenseness in his body released and his praises continued. "Good girl. That was..."

Lifting my face, I grinned. "Payback."

With his hands on both sides of my face, Damien lifted my lips to his. Strong and possessive as always, this kiss said more. It said that I was his and he was mine. It said I wasn't disappearing but growing.

When we came up for breath, I sat up and looked around. "Where are we?"

"I have no fucking idea."

We both laughed.

"I can be inappropriate too," I said.

"It's a deal. We can spend the rest of our lives trying to outdo one another, rekindling our desire."

"That sounds like a proposal. Was that a proposal, Mr. Sinclair?"

"One of many."

As I settled into my seat and buckled my seat belt, I had a thought that made me laugh.

"Private joke?" Damien asked.

"I was thinking I'm glad this dress is lined."

After repositioning himself, Damien leaned back, closing his pants and buckling his belt. "Next time, give me more of a heads-up. That seat belt was the death of me."

"Hmm."

His deep blue stare came my direction. "What?"

"Those toys you have," I said, speaking of the restraints, "now you know how I feel."

Damien's smile grew. "Frustratingly erotic."

"That about sums it up."

"Navigation," he said, speaking to the car, "home."

"You really don't know where we are?" I asked as the screen filled with the schematic of a map.

"I'm pretty sure I blacked out." He reached for my hand. "You're fucking amazing."

I tipped my head toward the screen. "Get us home and we can continue this celebration."

As Damien began to drive, it turned out we weren't too far off the beaten path. He had taken a few turns onto side streets and gotten us back into a neighborhood with big houses and large yards.

"Did Julia tell you why Dwain is leaving the coalition?" I asked.

"Competition policy. I'd expect that's with Sinclair. I don't care. I'm just glad he's out of it. Especially if he was involved in bugging our places. Good riddance."

"Do you think your car is bugged?"

We were now in familiar territory, heading home.

"If it is, they just got an earful." Damien looked my direction. "No, it isn't. After the nanny cams, I had our security company do a full sweep of our houses, cars, and offices."

"Dwain isn't leaving the coalition because of competition with Sinclair," I confided.

"Then why?"

"It has to do with a new venture, an offshoot of Moon Medical. Dwain Welsh is getting into the health-and brain-supplement market."

"Like Body Kindness?"

I nodded. "And he isn't doing it alone."

"Who is Dwain's new partner?"

Pressing my lips together, I turned toward the window.

"Are you clamming up on me now?"

"No." I turned and lifted my eyebrows. "I'm bargaining."

"You are?"

"If you can make me have one more orgasm when we get home, I'll tell you."

"Tell me now and I promise two or more."

I shook my head. "Confident."

"Very." Damien turned the SUV into our neighborhood. "Tell me."

"Darius."

His eyes widened. "No shit. Well, good. Hopefully, that will keep him away from Sinclair."

"I knew you'd be happy."

"I'll be happier when Duchess is watching us and you're screaming my name."

Chapter 32

Damien
Three months later

Dani straightened the bow tie of my tuxedo. Her blue gaze met mine. "I'm happy for you, big brother."

"We're going to do it right this time."

"Ella is right for you." Dani shrugged. "I'm not sure how you convinced her to give you another chance, but I'm glad you did."

At first, Jackie, Ella's mom, was unsure about my best man being a woman and Ella's maid of honor being a man, but somehow it felt right. Dani would stand with me and Niles with Ella. Ella's niece, Kenzie, was our flower girl.

With the help of her mother and some input from mine, our wedding was planned. More than planned. The day was here. There were no limits on what I would do for my wife-to-be. The biggest and most extravagant wedding was Ella's for the asking. Instead, with fewer than one hundred guests, we were to wed outside on a beautiful autumn day, surrounded by the oranges, reds, and yellows of changing leaves. Our reception will be in a beautifully restored barn. It even has a chandelier. According to Ella, similar venues were quite the rage these days.

"Do you have the wedding band?" I asked Dani.

"Oh damn." She turned right and left.

"One job."

Dani laughed, looking elegant in a slender black dress.

Black and white were our wedding colors. Ella said it was because life wasn't black and white. It made sense to her, so who was I to argue?

"I have it." Dani pulled the small box from her things. "You had plenty of time to get her a new band," she said, lifting Nana's ring.

"She didn't want a new one."

My sister grinned. "I love her." She playfully hit me. "If you screw this up, we're keeping her."

"Thanks. I don't plan on screwing it up."

There was a knock on our dressing room door. "Ella can't see you before the ceremony. I'll answer it," Dani said. After a peek, she opened the door wide. "Come in."

"We needed to see our son before his wedding," Mom said.

"Since we missed his first two," Dad said with a grin. He patted me on the shoulder. "We're proud of you, son. You're marrying the right one this time."

"I married the right one last time. It just wasn't legal."

Mom reached for my hand and for Dani's. "We're proud of both of you, and especially for how close you are." She inhaled. "I've been afraid to ask. Did you invite Darius?"

That had been an ongoing point of contention. "Ella said we should as a sign of good faith."

"You did?" Mom asked.

"Ella thought we should," I explained. "I figured since we weren't invited to his non-legal wedding to Amber, we could lose his invite. The final answer was no."

Dad nodded. "I understand. It still makes me sad."

"Not on our son's wedding day," Mom said, hugging Dad's arm.

"Are we going to do this?" Dani asked.

I looked at my watch. "It's about time."

"Ella is simply stunning," Mom said. "We stopped by her dressing room first."

"I wouldn't adhere to these stupid traditions if they weren't important to her."

Mom again reached for my hand. "That shows that you love her."

"I do. I really do."

After our parents left, I turned to Dani. "Thank you."

"I've got your back."

"And I've got yours."

Gabriella

"You're beautiful," Mom said as she adjusted the veil. "I'm so happy that we're with you for this special day."

"Me too, Mom. Things all worked out."

"They did," she said. "And Derek is looking healthy."

"Damien and I wanted you all to be here."

"And me," Kenzie said.

"You are beautiful, Gabby." My sister Charlotte was one of the few people who called me by another name. "And Kenzie has been practicing her petal drop." She turned to her daughter. "Are you ready?"

Kenzie nodded.

I reached for her shoulder. "Aunt Ella's got you."

"See, Mom. We're good."

I turned and met Niles's stare. "You're unusually quiet."

"I was just thinking," he said with a shimmer in his eyes. "You are visible, Ella. Definitely visible."

My lips quivered. "Don't you dare make me cry after that two-hour-long makeup session."

"I'm saving making you cry for my maid-of-honor speech."

"It's about time for the wedding," Mom said. "We'll be the ones in the front row."

"Thanks, Mom."

Charlotte and Mom left, leaving the four of us.

"What if I don't want to give you away," Dad asked, sporting a tuxedo.

"It's tradition. You're not really getting rid of me."

"Tradition," Niles said, looking dapper in his tuxedo. "Let's make sure we didn't forget anything. Old?" He began the roll call.

"My wedding band."

"New?"

I looked down at the long white gown. "My dress."

"Borrowed?"

Reaching up, I touched the pearl necklace my mother offered for me to wear. "Necklace."

"Blue?"

I tugged the hem of the dress, revealing my garter. "Covered."

Niles reached out his hand with something within his grasp. "And here, my friend, is a penny for your shoe. Jeremy wanted me to give it to you."

"You're the best."

I removed my foot and slipped the penny into the sole of my shoe.

Dad offered me his arm. "Come on, let's make this legal."

Legal.

I grinned. Yes, this time, our marriage would be legal.

We applied for the license together, and our officiant was here, ready to sign. What Florida hospital chaplain wouldn't accept an autumn trip to Indiana? I wanted Pastor Abrams to perform the ceremony, and Damien made it happen.

Niles was the first to walk down the aisle, followed by Kenzie in her white dress. As the music grew louder and the guests began to stand, Dad squeezed my hand. "I don't know what Niles was saying about you being visible, but according to this old man, Ella, you're the star. Damien's damn lucky to have you."

Lucky.

It all started with a lucky day.

No, on that day, it began to rekindle.

At the end of the aisle, my gaze met the navy-blue stare of my soon-to-be husband.

"We both are, Dad."

Epilogue

Gabriella
Spring of the following year

"I'm nervous," I admitted, overlooking an arrangement of appetizers. "Julia made this look so effortless."

Damien wrapped his arm around me and squeezed before snagging a cucumber from the vegetable tray. "Everything is perfect."

Perfect for the quarterly meeting of the pharma coalition. With caterers busy in the kitchen, I looked down at my long gown that my husband had chosen for this occasion. Soon, our home would be filled with all the people I'd met a year ago.

The Shermans, Robert Ayers and his new wife—his fifth, the Holstons, Cynthia Broche and her husband, Ian Morrison, the Cades, and of course, the Sinclairs. With Robert's new wife, we were at the same number as last year. However, we were without Dwain Welsh.

"So much has happened in the last year," I said.

"And next week is Beta Kappa Phi's annual gala. Mr. Phillips can suck it. Your dance card is full." Damien snaked his arm around me. "You're ravishing, Mrs. Sinclair. I can't wait to unzip this zipper."

"Anticipation. I draw the line at inappropriateness in the presence of your colleagues."

"Johnathon was outside my office..." Damien's eyebrows danced.

"Yeah," I said with a grin. "I'm glad he didn't come in the office."

"As long as you did."

Warmth filled my cheeks. "You know I did." My breathing hitched at the memory of being over Damien's desk. I may not work for him, but there were some workplace fantasies that refused to die.

The doorbell rang.

"Our guests are arriving," I said.

"Is it bad that I'm ready for them to leave?"

"Inappropriate..."

And they lived happily ever after!

Thank you for reading the Sinclair Duet. If you loved

Gabriella and Damien, be on the watch for Dani and Eli's story in Sinclair Duet II, a body-guard romance.

If you enjoyed the Sinclair Duet, check out the Sin Series (Donovan and Julia Sherman's story). Begin the binge today with **RED SIN**

What to do now

LEND IT: Did you enjoy REKINDLING DESIRE? Do you have a friend who'd enjoy REKINDLING DESIRE? REKINDLING DESIRE may be lent one time. Sharing is caring!

RECOMMEND IT: Do you have multiple friends who'd enjoy my dark romance with twists and turns and an all new sexy and infuriating anti-hero? Tell them about it! Call, text, post, tweet...your recommendation is the nicest gift you can give to an author!

REVIEW IT: Tell the world. Please go to the retailer where you purchased this book, as well as Goodreads, and write a review. Please share your thoughts about REKINDLING DESIRE:

*Amazon, REKINDLING DESIRE, Customer Reviews

*Barnes & Noble, REKINDLING DESIRE, Customer Reviews

*Apple Books, REKINDLING DESIRE Customer Reviews

* BookBub, REKINDLING DESIRE Customer Reviews

*Goodreads.com/Aleatha Romig

Books by ALEATHA

ALL AVAILABLE TO READ ON KINDLE UNLIMITED

IN PROGRESS:

SINCLAIR DUET:

REMEMBERING PASSION

September 2023

REKINDLING DESIRE

October 2023

ROYAL REFLECTIONS SERIES:

RUTHLESS REIGN

November 2022

RESILIENT REIGN

January 2023

RAVISHING REIGN

April 2023

READY TO BINGE:

SIN SERIES:

RED SIN

October 2021

GREEN ENVY

January 2022

GOLD LUST

April 2022

BLACK KNIGHT

June 2022

STAND-ALONE ROMANTIC SUSPENSE:

SILVER LINING

October 2022

KINGDOM COME

November 2021

DEVIL'S SERIES (Duet):

DEVIL'S DEAL

May 2021

ANGEL'S PROMISE

June 2021

WEB OF SIN:

SECRETS

October 2018

LIES

December 2018

PROMISES

January 2019

TANGLED WEB:

TWISTED

May 2019

OBSESSED

July 2019

BOUND

August 2019

WEB OF DESIRE:

SPARK

Jan. 14, 2020

FLAME

February 25, 2020

ASHES

April 7, 2020

DANGEROUS WEB:

Prequel: "Danger's First Kiss"

DUSK

November 2020

DARK

January 2021

DAWN

February 2021

* * *

THE INFIDELITY SERIES:

BETRAYAL

Book #1

October 2015

CUNNING

Book #2

January 2016

DECEPTION

Book #3

May 2016

ENTRAPMENT

Book #4

September 2016

FIDELITY

Book #5

January 2017

* * *

THE CONSEQUENCES SERIES:

CONSEQUENCES

(Book #1)

August 2011

TRUTH

* * *

STAND ALONE MAFIA THRILLER:

PRICE OF HONOR

Available Now

* * *

STAND-ALONE ROMANTIC THRILLER:

ON THE EDGE

May 2022

***

THE LIGHT DUET:

Published through Thomas and Mercer Amazon exclusive

INTO THE LIGHT

June 2016

AWAY FROM THE DARK

October 2016

TALES FROM THE DARK SIDE SERIES:

INSIDIOUS

(All books in this series are stand-alone erotic thrillers)

Released October 2014

* * *

ALEATHA'S LIGHTER ONES:

PLUS ONE

Stand-alone fun, sexy romance

May 2017

ANOTHER ONE

Stand-alone fun, sexy romance

May 2018

ONE NIGHT

Stand-alone, sexy contemporary romance

September 2017

A SECRET ONE

April 2018

MY ALWAYS ONE

Stand-Alone, sexy friends to lovers contemporary romance

July 2021

QUINTESSENTIALLY THE ONE

Stand-alone, small-town, second-chance, secret baby
contemporary romance

July 2022

ONE KISS

Stand-alone, small-town, best friend's sister,
grump/sunshine contemporary romance.

July 2023

* * *

INDULGENCE SERIES:

UNEXPECTED

August 2018

UNCONVENTIONAL

January 2018

UNFORGETTABLE

October 2019

UNDENIABLE

August 2020

ABOUT THE
AUTHOR

Aleatha Romig is a New York Times, Wall Street Journal, and USA Today bestselling author who lives in Indiana, USA. She has raised three children with her high school sweetheart and husband of over thirty years. Before she became a full-time author, she worked days as a dental hygienist and spent her nights writing. Now, when she's not imagining mind-blowing twists and turns, she likes to spend her time with her family and friends. Her other pastimes include reading and creating heroes/anti-heroes who haunt your dreams!

Aleatha impresses with her versatility in writing. She released her first novel, CONSEQUENCES, in August of 2011. CONSEQUENCES, a dark romance, became a bestselling series with five novels and two companions released from 2011 through 2015. The compelling and epic story of Anthony and Claire Rawlings has graced more than half a million e-readers. Her first stand-alone smart, sexy thriller INSIDIOUS was next. Then Aleatha released the five-novel INFIDELITY series, a romantic suspense saga, that took the reading world by storm, the final book landing on three of the top bestseller lists. She ventured into traditional publishing with Thomas and Mercer. Her books INTO THE LIGHT and AWAY FROM THE DARK were published through this mystery/thriller publisher in 2016.

In the spring of 2017, Aleatha again ventured into a different genre with her first fun and sexy standalone romantic comedy with the USA Today bestseller PLUS ONE. She continued the "Ones" series with additional standalones, ONE NIGHT, ANOTHER ONE, MY ALWAYS ONE, and QUINTESSENTIALLY THE ONE. If you like fun, sexy, novellas that make your heart pound, try her "Indulgence series" with UNCONVENTIONAL. UNEXPECTED, UNFORGETTABLE, and UNDENIABLE.

In 2018 Aleatha returned to her dark romance roots with SPARROW WEBS. And continued with the mafia romance DEVIL'S DUET, and most recently her SIN series.

You may find all Aleatha's titles on her website.

Aleatha is a "Published Author's Network" member of the Romance Writers of America and PEN America. She is represented by SBR Media and Dani Sanchez with Wildfire Marketing.

facebook.com/aleatharomig

twitter.com/aleatharomig

instagram.com/aleatharomig

Made in the USA
Monee, IL
08 March 2024

54720894R00174